SEVEN DAYS TO SILENCE

STORY OF RISHIKA

NAVEEN K. SHUKLA

Made with ♥ on the Notion Press Platform
www.notionpress.com

Prologue

People say time heals everything, but for me, time is just a reminder of how alone I am. My name is Rishika Kapoor, and sometimes I wonder if anyone would notice if I disappeared from this city.

I sat alone on the balcony of my flat, surrounded by the distant hum of Bengaluru's chaos. My eyes rested on the areca palm planted in a small pot, the one Chirag had planted for me. I reached out and brushed the leaves gently, my mind drowning in thoughts. How did it all come to this? I never imagined things would end this way. It was over. Everything was over.

The faint smell of Cuban cigar smoke broke through my thoughts. Startled, I looked up. My heart stopped. There he was—on the balcony right next to mine, standing exactly where I had first seen him, smiling with his piercing brown eyes, a cigar between his fingers. Fear gripped me like ice.

I knew why he was here. He must have known. Why would a murderer spare the girl who told the police about him? I wanted to run, but my legs wouldn't move. Before I could even try, his voice cut through the tension like a knife.

"Stop, Rishika!"

I froze. Slowly, I turned back to face him. He took a long drag from his cigar, then exhaled the smoke in my direction.

His voice was calm, but it carried a razor-sharp edge.

"Don't go anywhere," he said, his eyes locked onto mine. "I don't have much time."

My legs were trembling, but I gathered all my courage and spoke, "The police are after you."

"I know," he replied, his lips curling into a calm smile. "And it's all because of you."

Then, why was he here? I thought he'd already left the city, that he'd be at the railway station, bus stand, or maybe the airport. Why come here?

After a shaky breath, I forced out the question: "If you know the police are after you, why did you come here?"

"Where else would I go?" he said, his voice cold and steady. "Where else would I go... for this task?"

Task? What task? The realization hit me like a bolt of lightning. He was here to kill me.

My heart raced, thundering in my chest, as a cold sweat ran down my back. Everything suddenly made sense.

He slid his right hand into the pocket of his blue denim jacket. My heart pounded—I was sure he had a 9mm pistol in there. He was going to kill me. I squeezed my eyes shut, waiting for the end. So, this was it.

But then... nothing happened.

When he pulled his hand out, it wasn't a gun. Instead, it was an old Nokia phone. He powered it on, and the familiar start-up tune played. The sound took me back to my childhood, to the days when I used to switch my dad's phone on and off just to hear that tone.

He placed the phone on the edge of the balcony railing, the orange glow of his cigar lighting up his face. "I made it easy for them," he said, his voice calm, almost detached. "The police will find me soon. They'll track this phone." He took another drag, letting the smoke curl around him like a ghost.

I remembered he had told me once how his number was already on the police's radar, linked to a trail of crimes. "The moment I turn it on, they'll come for me," he'd explained.

Even now, I couldn't understand him. I rubbed my temples, confusion and fear swirling in my mind. "Why are you doing this?" I finally asked, my voice shaky.

He didn't answer immediately. He just looked out at the dark skyline, his face unreadable. Then, in that deep voice I once loved so much, he said, "Do me a favor."

"A favor?" I asked, unsure where this was going. "What kind of favor?"

"Play the violin, the tune which I taught you," he said simply, his tone soft but commanding.

"Violin?" I stammered, caught completely off guard.

"Yes," he said, taking another puff. "Play for me the tune. One last time... before they come."

His eyes looked far away, lost in thoughts I couldn't reach.

I couldn't figure him out. Was he waiting for me to play music before killing me? Gathering my courage, I asked, "Aren't you going to kill me?"

He laughed softly. "Kill you? How could I do that? Maybe you don't remember, but I saved your life once, right here. Now stop wasting time and play."

His words confused me, but I did as he said. I went inside, picked up my violin, and returned to the balcony. Standing in front of him, I placed the violin under my chin, gripped the bow, and began to play.

As the gentle notes filled the night air, the past few days replayed in my mind like a movie. Tears started streaming down my cheeks, and I didn't know why. Who was he to me? A murderer. That's all he was. But still, the emotions were too much for me to handle.

I kept my eyes closed, but I knew he hadn't left. The faint smell of his cigar lingered in the cool air. He stayed quiet, listening to every note. I knew the police were on their way. Any moment now, they'd burst in. But he didn't try to escape. He just stood there, still as a statue, listening to the music.

Who was this man? What kind of person listens to music while waiting to get caught?

My hands slowed, the music fading into silence. Sirens wailed in the distance, growing louder with each passing second. My heart pounded like a drum. Could I help him hide? Should I? He was a murderer.

"Don't stop!" His voice cut through my panic. It made me shiver. "Keep playing!"

I obeyed, my fingers shaking as they touched the violin strings. The melody was shaky, but I kept going. Two police cars screeched to a stop far below. I heard heavy boots pounding up the stairs. They were coming closer. Too close. Why wasn't he running? Why wasn't he trying to escape?

I glanced at him. He was smiling—calm, even amused. The cigar in his hand was almost gone, and he tossed it aside carelessly and then....

CHAPTER I

8th October, Thursday.

I met him on the night I planned to end my life. My plan was simple: jump from my balcony on the ninth floor. I even had two shots of whiskey to gather courage. I was just about to step off.

Then I smelled it—a rich, smoky scent, cutting through the fog in my mind. It was the smell of a Cuban cigar, something I had never experienced before, but a scent I would soon recognize well.

I turned slowly toward the balcony next to mine. At first, I wasn't sure what I saw. A tall figure stood there, shrouded in shadows. My heart skipped a beat. Was it a person? A ghost? Or is my imagination playing tricks on me?

I blinked, but he didn't disappear. He was real. There was no light on his balcony, only the dim glow from a distant streetlamp that outlined his figure. He was watching me, standing still, like he had been there forever, waiting for this exact moment.

"Are you going to jump?" he asked, his voice deep and smooth. "It doesn't suit a beautiful girl like you to end her life." His words struck me, but I wasn't about to be swayed by some stranger.

"None of your business," I snapped, my voice cold and harsh.

He took another puff of his cigar, and I found myself strangely calm in the midst of the smoke. I didn't even tell him to stop. Oddly enough, I didn't mind the smell.

"Please, don't do this," he said softly, stepping closer to the edge of his balcony. "Life is hard, I get it. But this isn't the answer."

As he moved into the faint light, I could finally see his face. He looked like he was in his late twenties, with rough features, a bit of a beard, and dark eyes. A strand of hair fell across his face, and he brushed it back with a casual flick of his hand. For some reason, I felt like he did that often as if it was a habit.

I couldn't help but find him interesting. Maybe, just for a moment, my plan could wait. I moved closer to the edge of my balcony until we were facing each other, just five feet apart.

"Don't give me those motivational speeches," I said, leaning on the railing. "I've been watching them on YouTube for two weeks, and none of them helped. My mind's made up."

As I leaned in to argue, I forgot what my landlord had told me—that the railing wasn't strong enough to hold much weight and needed repairs. Of course, he never got around to fixing it.

Suddenly, the railing gave way, and I felt myself falling, plummeting toward the ground. In that split second, I thought, *So, this is it, Rishika.*

But then, something stopped me – a strong hand grabbed my left arm. I wasn't falling anymore. I looked up, and there he was, leaning over his railing, holding onto me with all his strength. His other hand clutched the edge of the balcony, and I could see the strain in his biceps as he held me up.

Barely able to speak, I whispered, "Please, save me. I don't want to die."

"I won't let you die," he said firmly.

He began pulling me up, inch by inch until I finally reached his balcony. With his help, I managed to jump over the railing. I landed right on top of him, knocking him to the floor.

It was an awkward moment, to say the least. I could feel his heart pounding against my chest. My hair had fallen across his face, and my hands rested on his broad chest. My own heart was racing. I lifted my head to look at him and brushed my hair away. His deep brown eyes stared back at me. We were so close that I could feel the warmth of his breath on my skin.

A loud thunderstorm started outside, and without thinking, I wrapped my arms around him. Suddenly, I felt his hand gently resting on my back, and I realized what I had done. Embarrassment flooded my face. I didn't even want to look at him, but I knew I had to pull away.

When I finally looked at him, his expression was different—there was a strange hint of romance in it. He moved closer, and suddenly, the space between our lips felt almost non-existent. Was he going to kiss me?

I quickly stepped back, my heart racing. My mind screamed, "Don't kiss a stranger!" but my heart was thinking something else. Then, it started raining, pouring heavily over us. We were soaked and had no choice but to run inside from the balcony.

That's when I noticed something – I wasn't in my own flat. I was in his.

The entire memory hit me at once. I had been falling from my balcony, and this stranger saved me by pulling me onto his. He had jumped across a five-foot gap between our balconies, risking his life to save mine.

"Here, take this towel and dry yourself," he said, snapping me out of my thoughts. As I wiped myself, I caught a whiff of his scent, and it stirred something in me. I was angry at myself. How much trouble had I caused him?

Before I could apologize, he smiled and calmly asked, "Would you like some black coffee?" The soft light from the table lamp in his room highlighted his wheat-colored skin.

I nodded.

He went into the kitchen, which was just across the room, while I stood there, looking around. The room was small, and there wasn't much furniture. On one side, there was a single bed pushed against the wall. Next to it stood a desk. There were also two closets for clothes and two chairs for sitting. Despite its size, the room felt cozy and comfortable.

There was a typewriter on his desk. A typewriter, in this age of computers? Strange. A violin hung on the wall, and there was a photo of him shooting a pistol—maybe he was into competitions. I noticed a box of Cuban cigars on his bedside table.

Curiosity got the best of me. "Who are you?" I called out loudly enough for him to hear from the kitchen. "A writer with a typewriter? A violinist? A shooter?"

"I'm all of them—a writer, a violinist, and a shooting champion," he replied, walking back with two mugs of coffee.

The wind from the rainstorm outside blew into the room, making it feel cozy despite the weather. I picked up one of the coffee mugs. As soon as I smelled it, I realized it was different from the coffee I usually had. It didn't have that usual bitter coffee smell. I took a sip and couldn't help but exclaim, "Wow! This is amazing! I've never had black coffee like this before."

"You're very welcome," he replied with a smile.

"Tell me, what's in this amazing coffee?" I asked, curious about the secret.

"Just ginger and mint. They cut down the bitterness. That's all."

"Wow!" I said again, appreciating him as I took another sip.

He stared at me, his eyes full of something I couldn't quite place. Maybe attraction? We girls have a sixth sense for these things, but I didn't want the conversation to go there.

"Thank you... for saving my life."

"Your life was worth saving."

"I was out of my mind, thinking about ending it. But when I started falling..." I shivered, remembering hanging off the ninth floor.

"Don't think about it. Focus on moving forward," he said gently.

"Thanks again. I'm sorry, I didn't even ask your name."

"I'm Chirag... Chirag Kelkar," he said, extending his hand for a handshake.

"I'm Rishika Kapoor," I replied, shaking his hand. A strange current ran through me at his touch. Trying to shake it off, I asked, "So, Chirag, how come I've never seen you before? We live in flats right next to each other."

A hint of disappointment flashed across his face. "You don't remember me? We met just yesterday morning outside your flat."

"Did we?" I asked, confused.

He smiled and explained, "It was around 8:30 in the morning. You came out of your flat wearing a light yellow top and blue jeans. You were in a hurry, locking your door and holding a red envelope. You handed it to your landlord, saying, 'Here's the rent for the month,' and then you smiled at him. I was standing right next to him."

I felt a shock of embarrassment. He was right—I had handed the rent to the landlord yesterday morning. And now I remembered—a man had been standing next to him. It was Chirag.

"I'm sorry. I was rushing to catch my office cab. I didn't notice you at all."

"It's alright," he said, smiling. "I was there to check out this flat. Your landlord owns it, too. At first, I didn't want to take it."

"Why did you change your mind?" I asked, curious.

"I figured living next to a beautiful girl was a good enough reason to stay," he said with a grin.

I blushed, turning to look at the rain outside, which showed no sign of stopping. While taking a sip of the coffee, I asked, "So, what do you do for a living? You mentioned you're a writer, a violinist, and a shooter."

He chuckled and replied, "I'm a writer but with an old-fashioned typewriter."

"Why use a typewriter when you could use a computer?" I asked, genuinely curious.

"I like the noise it makes," he explained, mimicking the sounds with his mouth. "The rhythmic 'tap-tap-tap' as the keys hit, followed by a 'ding' when the line ends, and the quick 'zip' as the carriage slides back."

He made all the sounds, and it looked so funny that I thought he was *definitely a bit weird.*

"You're a writer by profession," I said, remembering his name. "Chirag Kelkar, right? What have you written? Where can I read your books?"

With a small cough and a bit of hesitation, he admitted, "Well, I'm not published yet. But in a couple of months, you'll find my book. You see, I used to be a ghostwriter. I wrote for others, but now I'm writing my own book. I've been in touch with a big publishing house. They'll publish it if they like my work. That's why I left Mumbai and came here—to focus on my book."

"All the best with your book!" I cheered, though I couldn't help but wonder if he had any real story ideas. So, I asked, "What's your book about? What genre do you like?"

"I'm writing a romantic thriller," he said. "Love stories with a touch of suspense."

"Do you have any specific story in mind?"

He looked into my eyes as if trying to draw me into his world, then turned toward the balcony, watching the rain pour outside. "On a stormy night, a beautiful girl meets a stranger. She falls in love, only to later discover that he's a killer."

I cringed. I couldn't hide my disappointment. "That's so boring! I've seen that story everywhere—TV shows, web series, audiobooks. It's been done to death!"

He took a long sip from his coffee, placed the mug on the table, and said with a grin, "Okay, let's flip the idea. A stranger meets a beautiful girl on a stormy night, falls in love with her, and later finds out *she's* the killer."

DONG... DONG...

The sound of the clock striking two echoed, and my heart skipped a beat.

"Oh no! It's already 2 AM. I'm so late! I have work tomorrow. I need to hurry!" I quickly placed the coffee mug on his desk and rushed toward the main door through the small living room. But just as I was about to leave, the power went out. The entire flat was plunged into complete darkness.

I froze. Fear gripped me. I had no idea what to do.

Then, from behind me, I heard a strange voice. It wasn't human. It was the kind of voice you hear in horror movies—unnatural and chilling.

"You can't leave this flat... ever. You're trapped here for the rest of your life."

Cold sweat trickled down my forehead. My heart pounded. I didn't dare turn around. What would I even see in this darkness? The storm outside only made it worse, and now, everything felt like a nightmare.

I was right about him – he wasn't human. He was a ghost.

CHAPTER II

9th October, Friday.

The next day, even though I woke up later than usual, I found myself smiling. I couldn't even remember the last time I had woken up with a smile on my face. It was all because of my neighbor, Chirag. I had been living in this city for around four years, renting different places, but I had never come across such an interesting neighbor before.

As I got ready for the office, I couldn't stop smiling, thinking about the prank Chirag had pulled the night before. He was such a funny guy and great at making mimicry sounds. Last night, when there was a power cut at his flat, he made this creepy, horrible noise that had me convinced for a moment that he was a ghost living in the abandoned flat next to mine.

When I finally realized it was just a prank, I was furious. He had no idea how scared I was! I even wanted to strangle him for scaring me like that.

As I was leaving for work and locking my door, I thought of saying "hello" to Chirag to thank him for making my morning so cheerful. But to my surprise, I saw a lock hanging on his door. Where could he have gone this early in the morning? He had told me he wasn't working anywhere and was just staying in the city to write his novel. Oh well, I shrugged it off and hurried to catch my office cab.

I lived in Blue Sky Apartment in Brookfield. At 8:30, I had to catch my office cab to get to work. With my headphones on and eyes closed, I tried to block out the usual city traffic—the same buildings, shops, schools, and people. I liked listening to podcasts of start-up founders during my ride.

It had always been my dream to start my own company after completing my B. Tech from Delhi, I came to this city with hopes of launching a start-up. In fact, I started four different ones, but all of them failed, leaving me with a mountain of debt. To pay off my loans, I took a job as a developer at Zenith Networks. The job didn't give me much satisfaction, but it helped me cover my EMIs—well, most of them, anyway. I still struggled to pay some regularly.

When the cab stopped, we reached the commercial complex in Whitefield, where my office was located on the fifth floor.

While waiting for the elevator to my office, I ran into Sara. She was my best friend at work. Sara had a round face, chubby cheeks, and curly hair. Her cheeks were so soft that you always wanted to squish them. She was a local, born and raised in the city, and had been my biggest support since I moved here.

"Hey, Sara!" I greeted her.

"Hi, Rishi," she replied. Sara always called me "Rishi" instead of "Rishika" because we liked giving each other funny, short nicknames.

"How was your Tinder date last night?" I asked. Sara loved using dating apps to find someone special.

"Don't even ask," she said with a playful sigh. "I can't believe how rude people on Tinder are these days."

"But what happened?" I asked, curious.

"Forget it, Rishi," she said as the elevator doors opened. We stepped in. In the crowded elevator, she continued, "My mood was so off after that stupid date. I called you to hang out at

Galaxy, but your phone kept ringing. You didn't answer. Did you fall asleep early?"

Galaxy was a disco bar we often visited to chill out.

"Yeah, I had a really bad headache, so I went to bed early," I lied.

The truth was, when she called, I was standing on my balcony, contemplating jumping off to end my life. But I didn't want to share that with her. No one wants to hear stuff like that. Plus, she'd probably drag me back to Dr. Neelam, the city's famous psychiatrist, for more sessions. I had seen Dr. Neelam during my depression, but I was fine now and didn't want to go back.

While I was lost in my thoughts, Sara suggested I try some Ayurvedic oil for headaches. I nodded without even catching the name of the oil.

The elevator stopped on the fifth floor, and we walked into the office after punching our cards. That's when the bomb dropped. Our colleague, J.K., informed us that Mr Deshmukh was going to hold a project meeting with our client present.

"Oh no, Sara, please stop this meeting! I can't stand Mr Deshmukh's meetings. He's so boring," I groaned.

"Don't be silly. We all have to deal with it. But what can we do? Deshmukh is the project head. I can't exactly tell him, 'Please, sir, don't have the meeting because we have headaches,' can I?"

Jokingly, I said, "Sara, please order that Ayurvedic oil you mentioned earlier. Ship it to the office. I need it right now!"

Three hours later, we were sitting in the conference room. Mr. Deshmukh, our project head, was giving a serious presentation about the client's demands and the roadmap for our upcoming project.

Deshmukh was very serious about the project. Our new assignment was from a prestigious university in North India. They wanted us to create software for their online student counseling and admissions. I knew how important the project was because our company's reputation was on the line. But Deshmukh made everything feel even more intense.

He was a bald man with a belly, in his late forties, always wearing a serious expression. Even at his own birthday party, he was the only one who looked so serious. During the project presentation, he repeated the same thing three—no, four times—each time ending with his favorite phrase, "Isn't it?"

After that long meeting, all of us colleagues began jokingly saying "Isn't it?" to each other. The work could have been finished soon, maybe even today.

But today felt different for me. Before coming to the meeting, I promised myself I wouldn't get bored. To avoid it, I started recalling some funny things. As the meeting began, I tried thinking of jokes, and eventually, my mind wandered to last night's prank by my new neighbor, Chirag. His mischievousness made me smile. I didn't even realize that Deshmukh had noticed me grinning.

Sara, who was sitting next to me, noticed me smiling like a fool. She tapped my leg with hers as a warning, but I ignored her and kept doing it anyway.

Mr Deshmukh noticed. His sharp eyes focused on me as he said, "Rishika, would you mind outlining our new project for everyone?" His tone was just as sharp.

With Deshmukh's order, I wouldn't say I was scared, but I definitely wasn't smiling anymore. I stood up, pretending I had been paying full attention the whole time. I confidently walked over to the projector and switched it off, then turned on the room lights. Everyone watched as I moved the whiteboard from the corner of the room to the center.

I grabbed a black marker and drew the project outline, the same one I had made last month with just a few tweaks. I explained everything clearly, pointing out each detail. Our demanding client was in the room, and to my surprise, he looked impressed. When I finished, everyone clapped.

Mr Deshmukh wasn't pleased. His face was tight, knowing he had lost the chance to humiliate me yet again.

As everyone was leaving the room, he came up to me and whispered so only I could hear, "I know you're the best at what you do, Rishika, but stop smiling during meetings. It's distracting."

I chuckled softly. After he left, Sara came over and teased, "Girl, what are you doing? You're always teasing Mr. Deshmukh with that smile of yours."

"I wasn't teasing him! My smile had nothing to do with him," I replied, still smiling.

"Oh? Then tell me, why were you smiling so much?" Sara questioned.

I joked, "I'll tell you, but only in the canteen because I'm starving! After this boring meeting with Deshmukh, I feel like rats are eating away at my stomach."

Sara, always a foodie, agreed immediately. We rushed to the canteen on the ground floor of the complex. We ordered burgers and water bottles, then looked for a quiet spot to sit and chat. We found a corner table and settled down.

Sara was curious about why I was smiling. She grinned and said, "Tell me, did you join a dating app again like I suggested? Is that why you're smiling?"

I shook my head. "No, it's not that. I'm done with dating apps." The last time I used one, I met Chetan. After our breakup, I deleted the app and never went back.

"Then what is it?" Sara asked, grabbing her burger. She looked cute, with her cheeks puffed out from the big bite she took.

"I've been smiling because of my neighbor—Chirag!" I said.

As soon as I mentioned Chirag, something changed. Sara's face went pale, and she suddenly started coughing. Bits of the burger came flying out of her mouth. She looked ridiculous. I quickly handed her the water bottle, and she gulped down a lot of water, her eyes red from choking on the food.

"Are you okay?" I asked.

"Yeah," she said, standing up from the chair. "I need to go back to my desk. I have important work to do."

What just happened? I wanted to say something, but before I could, she rushed off to the elevator. I was left sitting there alone. I looked around and noticed that everyone else was sitting with their friends or colleagues. Only I was sitting alone now.

Sara was acting strange. What did I say? Why did she get so weird when I mentioned Chirag? Then I remembered that stormy night when I stayed over at Sara's place. We were sharing her bed, and out of nowhere, she started kissing me passionately. When I pushed her away, she apologized.

Did Sara have feelings for me? Is that why she didn't want any guy in my life? I had even wondered if she had something to do with my breakup with Chetan.

Whatever. I wasn't going to let her ruin my mood. I still had my burger to enjoy—even if I was eating it alone.

I returned to my desk after lunch. On my way back, I noticed Sara sitting at her desk, talking to someone on the phone. So, that was her important work—chatting away with someone. She didn't even glance in my direction. I acted like I hadn't seen her either. Besides, I had way too much work to do. I had to write a ton of code for the project, conduct a training session for the juniors, and prepare a presentation.

My phone buzzed, pulling me away from my coding. As annoying as it was, I had to check it - who can resist looking at their phone notifications? It was a message from Dr Neelam inviting me to her wedding anniversary party tonight at Hotel Padmini Inn. Weird, right? I mean, who invites their patients to their wedding anniversary? I couldn't help but think that maybe Dr Neelam had lost her mind while treating all of her mindless patients.

I wasn't planning on going anywhere tonight.

At seven, I left my desk, swiped my card, and waited by the elevator. Suddenly, I felt a tap on my shoulder. It was Sara. She looked... different this time. She was more normal, not her usual weird self. She smiled politely, and I did the same. I wasn't in the mood to bring up her strange behavior in the canteen earlier.

"So, are you coming?" she asked after clearing her throat.

"Where?"

"To Dr. Neelam's party. I thought she might have invited you too."

"Yes, I got the invite, but I'm not going."

"Why? Come on, Rishi, we'll have fun at the party," she said it so casually, like she always did when she wanted me to join her in her plans.

"I still can't understand why my psychiatrist is inviting me to her wedding anniversary party. She must have hundreds of patients. Is she inviting all of them?"

"She didn't invite you because you're her patient. She invited you because you're like family to her."

"I'm not family, but you are."

Sara's father was a famous criminal lawyer, and he had connections with many prominent people in the city, including Dr. Neelam. Sara was practically family to her.

"But you're my friend, and that makes you my family too," Sara said, sounding all innocent, completely unaware of how she had treated me just hours before in the canteen when I had tried to share my feelings about someone special.

But I didn't say anything to Sara about what happened in the canteen. I was so tired and had no energy left to argue with her. In a firm voice, I simply said, "No, I won't come."

Then, the elevator arrived, and I quickly got in without checking if Sara was behind me or not. There was a small crowd trying to get into the lift. Once inside, I saw Sara standing at the door.

When the lift reached the ground floor, I walked out, ignoring Sara, who was busy chatting with some colleagues at the door. I headed straight toward my office cab, but just as I was about to sit, Sara called out from behind. I was irritated this time, so I snapped at her, "What?"

Since we're friends and know each other's moods well, Sara quickly realized I was annoyed. She spoke softly, "If you come to the party, Dr. Neelam would be happy to see you."

I didn't respond and just got into the cab.

CHAPTER III

"Stop!" I yelled at the cab driver, who was blasting music from the speakers. "I said stop right here!"

The tires screeched as he hit the brakes. I grabbed my handbag and stepped out.

"Madam, you're always getting off here these days. This isn't your usual stop; it's two kilometers away from your apartment," the cab driver said, laughing unnecessarily, flashing his yellow, gutkha-stained teeth. He was a local guy—fat, with very dark skin, and always leering at women in short skirts or low-cut tops.

"Just do your job. It's none of your business," I snapped back at him.

Why was I really stopping there? I had spotted my handsome neighbor, Chirag, walking down the street. After the cab left, I kept an eye on Chirag, curious to see where he was headed.

It was late evening, and the street was buzzing with activity. There were shops, malls, and street food vendors, all lit up by neon signs and streetlights. Amid the noise of traffic and the crowd, I saw Chirag—walking like a hero, smoking a cigar. The smoke made him stand out.

I had to cross the busy road to reach him. Waving my hand to signal cars and bikes to stop, I made my way across the zebra crossing. But by the time I reached the other side, he had disappeared from view. I hurried down the street and noticed a narrow road to my left. Without thinking, I turned down it.

It wasn't as crowded as the main road, but there were still shops and small markets. I wandered down the street, unsure of how far I should go to find him. And then, there he was.

Chirag was standing on the sidewalk under the shade of a small tree, still puffing on his cigar, intently watching a shop across the street—CredZone. The shop's neon glow signboard showed that it was a loan-providing company that provided loans to customers 24/7.

I walked up behind him quietly, trying not to disturb his focus. He was staring at the CredZone.

Why was he here? Did he want to get a loan?

"So, how was your day? How was the office?" he suddenly asked, but I wasn't sure who he was talking to. Then he turned to me. The streetlight above him cast a soft glow. He looked really good in his black round-neck T-shirt and blue jeans.

"Hello, I'm talking to you," he said, snapping me out of my thoughts about him.

"Do you have eyes on the back of your head?" I chuckled. "How did you know I was behind you?"

"I even knew you got out of your office cab on the main road," he replied.

I thought I was following him, but it seemed like he had been watching me all along.

"So, tell me," I asked, pointing to the building behind him, "why are you standing here in front of this lending company's office?"

Chirag leaned closer and said, "This company gives loans to people, and most of the time, they deal in cash. Imagine how much cash they must have locked away in their office safe."

His words made no sense to me. I frowned and asked, "So what? What's your point?"

"He's here to rob it," he said with a serious expression. "He wants to check the place out and make a plan."

"Who is he? A criminal?" I asked, feeling a bit nervous.

"He's a character in my novel," he explained, still serious.

"Your character is going to rob this company?" I asked, surprised.

"Yes."

"So, stop him."

"Why?"

"Why not? Robbing is a crime, and committing crimes is insane."

"But what about my story?"

"Don't write crime stories. Write about romance instead."

"I am writing romance," he said, "but my hero has a criminal mind. I can't change him."

He took one last drag of his cigarette, blowing smoke rings into the air before tossing it aside. I found myself getting more and more interested in his plot, even though I didn't know why. Talking to him was fun. "Does your hero think robbing is easy?" I asked.

"Yes, it's easy," he replied. "This place is on a deserted road. There are no big shops around, only some large bungalows that are usually empty. Late at night, the street is completely quiet. This office stays open till midnight. My hero plans to rob it late at night."

I laughed, "So, your hero's just going to stroll in and rob the place, waving his hands?"

But he wasn't laughing. He stayed serious. "He'll come with a gun in his pocket."

There was something strange in his brown eyes. A chill ran down my spine as fear crept in. Suddenly, I remembered the photo on the wall in his room. It showed him as a shooter, holding a gun.

Then, he burst out laughing. "You got scared!" he said, patting my shoulder. "Relax, it's just a story." He asked me, "By the way, what are you doing here?"

Oh no, I'd forgotten I was there too and that I had to explain why! What could I say? I quickly looked around, searching for a reasonable answer, and ended up saying, "You see that grocery shop? I often come here to buy some things. So I came today, and then I saw you standing here, so I walked over to you."

He smiled as if he knew I was lying and said, "Then let's go to your grocery shop."

We started walking toward the shop at the corner of the street. I panicked, realizing I had no actual reason to buy anything today. He kept smiling and said, "Don't you think this shop is a bit far from our apartment? I've noticed many shops much closer."

What could I say? I didn't want to admit the truth—that I was there just to see him, and I'd even gotten out of my cab two kilometers early just for him.

I changed the topic, asking, "You're not on social media, are you?"

He chuckled. "So, you searched for me online? That's nice, but no, I'm not there."

"Why not? Everyone's on social media these days."

"It distracts me. Messes with my focus, especially my writing."

By then, we'd reached the grocery store, walking side by side. I realized I hadn't even thought about what I needed to buy. I just mumbled random items to the shopkeeper, barely paying attention to whether I actually needed them. But I didn't want to look clueless in front of him.

The shopkeeper handed me a plastic bag with the groceries. I paid, and as we turned to leave, Chirag reached out to help me carry the bag.

"Don't you need anything?" I asked.

"Nah," he replied teasingly. "I usually buy groceries from the shops near our place, so I don't have to lug bags too far."

"Fine, then give me my bag. I'll carry it myself," I said, half annoyed but smiling. His teasing was getting to me.

He chuckled. "Sorry, sorry. I'll carry it wherever you need."

We both laughed and soon we reached the main road where we'd have to turn right for our apartment. The road was busy, headlights flashing, sometimes blinding us with their brightness.

Suddenly, a biker came racing toward me, weaving wildly. I froze, watching the bike come closer, my mind blank with fear. In an instant, Chirag pulled me out of harm's way, his strong grip steadying me as the bike sped past, missing me by an inch.

"Are you okay?" he asked, his eyes wide with concern.

My heart pounded, and my breath was shaky. He handed me a water bottle, and I took a few sips to calm down.

"Yes, I'm okay now," I managed, looking up at him. In his steady brown eyes, I found the safety and reassurance I hadn't felt in a long time.

We started our journey back to the apartment. Chirag suggested we take an auto after the bike incident, but I insisted we walk. The wind was gentle and cool, and we chatted about random topics, laughing at silly things—especially his jokes and the funny sounds he made.

At times, to avoid traffic, we had to walk so close that our fingers would brush against each other. Each time they touched, we'd pull them away—until he gently held my hand and looked into my eyes. This time, I didn't pull away. I took a deep breath.

Before I knew it, we'd reached our apartment. We took the elevator up to the ninth floor.

Chirag was so kind and thoughtful, carrying my shopping bags all the way without a single complaint. We finally stood outside my flat, which was locked. I unlocked the door, and we stepped inside. Although the walk hadn't tired me much, the sight of my cozy couch made me realize just how exhausted I was—I felt completely drained.

It was as if Chirag could read my mind. He looked at me and said, "You go freshen up; I'll make us some black coffee."

In my head, I thought, *Oh, Chirag, you're so thoughtful! I really needed that.* But aloud, I said, "No, Chirag, you must be tired too. You carried my shopping bags all the way. I'll make the coffee."

Chirag just smiled, pointing toward the bathroom, knowing I was only being polite. As I headed to freshen up, I heard his voice from the kitchen, "How about some sandwiches with the coffee?"

"I'd love that!" I replied, smiling.

What more could I ask for? Coming home after a long day with hot black coffee and the delicious smell of sandwiches waiting for me. I changed into my comfy night clothes and joined Chirag on the balcony. We sat together, enjoying the coffee, the breeze, and the lights of Bengaluru in the distance.

I took a bite of the sandwich and couldn't help but say, "This is amazing, perfectly cooked! Whenever I make sandwiches, they always seem to burn because I never know when to stop."

Chirag just smiled, saying nothing, but his warmth said it all.

As I ate my sandwich, I looked at Chirag and said, "Chirag, you're a writer, a violinist, a shooting champion, and, I must say, quite the chef too."

He grinned mischievously and replied, "And yours...?"

He left the sentence hanging, his smile playful. I knew what he wanted to say—*"And your lover?"*—or at least that's what I thought.

I played along. "And my...?"

Chirag leaned in, his eyes meeting mine. My heart raced. But with a laugh, he finished, "And your neighbor too."

He laughed heartily, and I felt embarrassed. Here I was, thinking he was about to confess his love, and all he meant was being my neighbor. Although he didn't say he loved me then, his eyes told me he did. Eyes don't lie. Was I being foolish to think that way?

I had only met him the day before, and here I was, wondering if it was love. I didn't know him well, and he didn't know me. How could two strangers feel love so quickly? These questions filled my mind, but my heart whispered, *This is love—when you see someone and something inside tells you that you've found the one you've been searching for.*

He placed his coffee cup on the balcony ledge after taking the last sip. He talked about random things, but my mind drifted, lost in my thoughts as I sipped the coffee and ate the sandwich he had made for me.

Suddenly, my phone buzzed on the bedside table inside the room. I didn't want to go in; I wanted to stay right there with him. When it stopped ringing after a few seconds, I felt relieved. But then it buzzed again. I finally went to check—it was Dr. Neelam. *Why was she calling at this hour, around ten at night?*

I ignored her call but kept staring at the screen, tempted to switch the phone off. Then a message

popped up,

"Hey Rishika, hope you're doing well! I sent an invite to the party. It would've been nice if you came! Goodnight."

I rolled my eyes at her message.

"Alright, goodnight then," I heard Chirag say. I turned to see him standing on the balcony ledge, waving goodbye. My heart skipped a beat, and my eyes went wide. Suddenly, he leaped off the ledge! I wanted to scream, but my throat felt tight. *Did he really do that?*

"Chirag!" I finally shouted and ran to the balcony, expecting to see him nine floors below, lying still on the ground. But instead, I saw him standing on his own balcony, smiling and waving up at me. He had jumped—not to the ground, but to his balcony five feet apart.

I caught my breath and glared at him. "Don't you think that was risky? You could've just gone to your flat through the main door!"

"Oh, come on! The main door is boring!" he laughed. "Jumping from your balcony to mine is way more exciting!"

He was still smiling, but I wasn't. I could barely breathe; my chest felt tight with relief and frustration. I said nothing, my mood darkened, and I turned to go inside. I heard him call my name, but I ignored it and went straight to my bed.

Then I heard a soothing violin tune—deep and heart-touching. The sound came from the next balcony. I closed my eyes and let myself drift into the music. My frustration melted away. I felt calm and at peace.

After a while, I stood on my balcony, watching him play the violin on his balcony. With a smile, I said, "So, do you think you can win me over with your violin?"

I wanted him to know I wasn't so easy to impress.

He paused, looked at me and said, "Alright then, what do you want? I'll do whatever you say."

"I want a treat from you," I replied.

He smiled and answered, "I'm ready. I'm in."

That night, as I lay in bed, I could hear the steady tap of his typewriter coming from his room. It wasn't annoying; it had a calming rhythm. I fell asleep with a smile on my face.

CHAPTER IV

10th October, Saturday.

The next day was Saturday, just a regular Saturday, not the weekend. When I first joined Zenith Networks, we had weekends on both Saturdays and Sundays. But, as you know, policies change often in IT companies. About six months ago, my boss, CMD Sir, announced that due to the increased workload, we'd only have a one-day weekend. He promised that once the workload decreased, we'd return to two-day weekends. But to be honest, that day never arrived. So, here I was, getting ready for work on a Saturday.

Despite working late hours on Saturdays, I actually liked them—it was my favorite day of the week. Saturdays always held the promise that a holiday was just around the corner. Even back in school, I loved Saturdays for that very reason. I enjoyed Sundays too, but Saturday was special because it meant freedom was near. By Sunday evening, though, the fun began to fade as I started dreading Monday. But today, I was happy because it was Saturday.

As I showered, my soap slipped from the case and fell, which made me think of last night. Chirag had taken a daring leap from my balcony to his, and I couldn't help but imagine what could have happened if he'd missed by even an inch. A shiver ran through me, just picturing him falling nine floors down. I shook my head to clear the thought, refocusing on the evening ahead. Chirag was going to treat me to make up for his wild jump. Could I call it a first date?

As I stepped out of my flat, locking the door behind me, I was surprised to see the lock hanging on Chirag's door. When did he leave each morning? The lock hanging outside meant he was already out. Odd, since I'd heard his typewriter clacking away through the night. Around 4 a.m., when I got up to use the washroom, the rhythmic tap-tap was still echoing through the walls. After working so late, he should've been asleep, not out and about. Strange. But I had no time to dwell on it; my cab would be here any moment.

My usual day started as I climbed into the cab, earbuds in, enjoying my favorite podcast on the way to the office. Suddenly, my phone buzzed. A message from Dr Neelam—again. What could she want now? I opened it, reading: *"Dear Rishika, I understand why you couldn't make it to my party last night; you must have been tired. But I'd love to catch up! Let's meet tonight at Cyrus' Corner, near your place, after work. I have a little return gift for you."*

A return gift? But I hadn't even attended her party! Well, no harm in stopping by. Cyrus's Corner was a cozy spot nearby, perfect for unwinding. I typed back, *"Alright, see you there."*

I punched my card and stepped into the office. Right there, in the middle of the corridor, I saw Sara chatting with a colleague. I gave her a polite, formal smile. But today, I was determined to keep things strictly professional. No gossip, no small talk. And definitely no mention of Chirag. Even if she brought him up, I'd stay cool. I walked past her, keeping my distance, and headed straight to my desk.

Of course, Sara soon followed. I could almost predict it, knowing her.

"Hi Rishi, are you okay now?" she asked.

I replied with a hint of irritation, "What happened to me?"

She hesitated, "I mean... your mood. Is it okay?"

"Whose mood would be okay working on a weekend day?" I shot back in the same tone.

She sighed, "True. Who knows when CMD sir will bring back two-day weekends."

I kept quiet, pretending to be too busy setting up my desktop and arranging paperwork to notice.

Then, after a pause, she ventured, "Yesterday's party at Dr. Neelam's was amazing! Her husband sang a beautiful song for—"

I cut her off, "Could you email me the Suzon project details as soon as possible?"

Her face fell, clearly disappointed that I wasn't interested in her story.
"Okay, I'll send it over," she mumbled, deflated, as she turned back to her desk, her sandals ticking on the floor like a clock counting down her disappointment.

I had to meet with HR Manager Kamini Duggal, a heavyset woman in her fifties. No idea why, but she always seemed to have a problem with me. She called me in to say that I hadn't attended an online training session led by some IT expert the previous Sunday.

I hated those sessions—especially when they were on Sundays.

"Everyone was present except you," she said, her glasses slipping down her nose as she gave me a stern look.

"I'll make sure I'm there next time," I replied, not knowing what else to say.

Then she launched into the same speech she always did about how important these training sessions were and how they opened up endless opportunities for us. I could probably recite her whole spiel by heart at this point—she used the exact same lines every time.

Sitting there, listening to her lecture, was torture. When would it end? She kept going, her hand waving in the air as she rattled off the same nonsense.

Finally, her phone rang. Thank God. I think it was a personal call because she waved me off to go back to my desk.

As usual, it happened again. After my meeting with HR, my mood was ruined. Frustrated and angry, I took it out on the trainees during our afternoon session.

I pointed out every little mistake they made and criticized their presentations over minor issues. I even yelled at them for simple errors in the code they had written. I let my anger loose, not holding back because I was tired, frustrated, and fed up. It was Saturday, and despite the weekend, I was still in the office.

On top of that, I was annoyed with my best friend, Sara. When I mentioned Chirag, she acted strangely, and I had no idea why. And then there was HR, Kamini Duggal. She didn't like me, and the feeling was mutual. Her meeting left me in an even worse mood. So, there I was, unloading all my frustration onto the trainees, hoping it would give me some relief.

Just then, my phone buzzed with a message. It was from Chirag. I want to *remind you that I owe you a party tonight!* The message ended with a smiley emoji.

I chuckled, and my worries seemed to disappear. It was like he knew I needed cheering up at that moment. I texted back, "Yep, I remember! See you at 8:00 at Cyrus's Corner."

Cyrus's Corner is a famous bakery and restaurant run by an old but lively Parsi man named Mr. Rustom Daruwalla. It's a cozy place where people love to hang out. The best part? It's just a short walk from my apartment.

That evening, around 8:25 PM, I headed there and found Chirag already sitting at a table in the middle, waiting for me. He didn't see me because the place was crowded. Even from a distance, I recognized him by the familiar swirl of cigar smoke he had around him. The smoke twisted and curled, forming a whirl around him, making him unmistakable even in the dim light.

It was the second weekend of the month, and a special musical performance by the Admas Band was scheduled. People eagerly looked forward to this event every month.

But I didn't want to go straight to Chirag right away. I slipped away to the washroom, wanting to freshen up and look my best before meeting him. I had my small makeup kit in my bag, just for moments like these. I quickly dabbed on some powder, added a hint of blush, and swiped on my pink lipstick. I brushed through my hair and fixed my eyeliner, feeling confident and ready.

When I finally approached Chirag, I could tell my quick makeover had worked. His mouth literally dropped open when he saw me.

"Are you inviting a fly into your mouth?" I teased, laughing at his surprised expression.

He blushed, and I thought, *Wow, this guy is shy.*

He pulled out a chair for me, which I appreciated – it was sweet and thoughtful. After what felt like ages, he finally spoke, "I thought you came straight from the office."

"Why do you ask?" I responded. "I did come straight from work."

"You look like you just walked out of a beauty parlor to kill every guy in this place," he chuckled.

This time, it was my turn to blush.

His cigar burned to the end, and he crushed it in the ashtray on the table. Curious, I asked, "What kind of cigar is this?"

"This?" He paused, then said, "It's Cuban."

It was the first time I realized his cigar was from Cuba.

"It looks expensive," I commented.

He nodded. "Yeah, it is. And it's not easy to find in India. That makes it even more costly."

"What? Is it not available in India? Then how do you get it?" I asked, surprised.

He chuckled and leaned in close. His breath, tinged with the scent of smoke, brushed against my face. His expression turned serious as if he was about to share a secret. "It's smuggled," he whispered, then pulled back.

I understood, but I had to ask, "Why take such a risk just for this?"

He smiled, glancing at the finished cigar in the ashtray. "I love it," he said. "You could say I'm hooked on this cigar."

We ordered a chocolate pastry and cold coffee. Chirag had never been to Cyrus' Corner before, so he looked around curiously, taking in the place. After a few moments, he gave me a smile, one that felt a little too romantic. I liked the attention, but I started feeling a bit self-conscious. To shift the mood, I said,

"You've never been here, but I'm sure you'll love it, especially the Admas Band tonight."

"Yeah, I've heard people talk about it. You seem pretty familiar with this place," he said.

"I know it well! Rustom uncle, the owner, knows me by name."

Chirag brushed the hair from his face with a casual flick, and I couldn't help but find him even cuter. He looked around at the crowded space and then said, "I had no idea this place would be so full. I'm sorry... Do you think we could find somewhere quieter for our first date?"

Wait... did he just say the first date? I wasn't sure I'd heard him right, but before I could ask, the waiter arrived with our order. I forgot what I was about to say and instead asked, "So, where do you go every morning?"

"What do you mean?" he asked.

"I mean, every morning when I leave for work, I see your door locked from outside."

He replied, "Every morning, I went to the gym near our apartment. I loved it."

I could tell it was true—his toned body showed the results of those workouts, especially his strong biceps. I still couldn't forget that night when he held my whole body, dangling from the balcony, with just one hand.

"And where do you get the energy for that? You stay up all night typing away on your typewriter."

He looked genuinely surprised. "How do you know I'm up writing all night?"

"I can hear the *tap-tap-tap* and the *zip* of your typewriter through the wall," I laughed.

He looked embarrassed. "Oh no! I'm sorry if the noise bothers you."

I waved it off. "Don't worry about it! I'm used to sleeping through all kinds of noise. I could probably sleep right here with all this chaos."

Suddenly, there was a bit of a commotion. I saw Mr. Daruwalla surrounded by a group of people who looked upset. Curious, Chirag and I went over to see what was happening. Mr. Daruwalla looked sad as he explained, "I know you're all waiting for the Adams Band, but unfortunately, they won't be performing tonight."

"What?!" I blurted, along with the rest of the crowd. The band was the main reason people had come, and now they were leaving disappointed.

Just then, Chirag surprised me. He stepped forward and asked Mr. Daruwalla, "If it's okay, could I play the violin to cheer people up?"

Mr. Daruwalla looked at Chirag with doubt in his eyes. But Chirag met his gaze, his face full of confidence. Seeing this, Mr. Daruwalla slowly nodded.

I had no idea Chirag had brought his violin. He had it with him the whole time, tucked beside his chair. My heart raced as he stepped up onto the stage. I was nervous—what if he didn't play well? How would people react?

Chirag stood confidently, the violin tucked under his chin. His fingers moved smoothly across the strings as the bow danced over them. The music that filled the room was full of energy and emotion. It soared, full of love, and pulled everyone in. It was as if the sound wrapped around us all, making everything feel lighter and more alive.

I couldn't explain it, but the music took me to another place. Couples started dancing, and I could see the smile on Mr. Daruwalla's face. Chirag was saving the evening.

I felt thrilled and proud watching Chirag's violin performance. This man had every quality a girl dreams of – he was strong, romantic, and had just the right mystery to drive a girl wild. And right then, I declared I was that kind of girl, completely swept away by him.

As soon as Chirag finished playing the violin, the crowd at Cyrus' Corner burst into cheers and applause. People gathered around him, celebrating alongside Mr. Daruwalla, clapping and shouting his name with excitement.

But just when I thought everything was perfect, my happiness faded.

I wanted to rush up and congratulate him, but then I saw him—Ramesh Reddy, a banker I knew too well.

He was there, front and center, and my heart sank. I needed to leave before he saw me. I was about to slip out when Chirag called my name. I froze. Ramesh had spotted me.

With an angry look on his face, he walked straight toward us.

He stood before us, yelling with an angry look in his dark eyes. His hand rested on his huge belly as he shouted, his voice booming around us, "Where the hell have you been, Rishika? You didn't answer my calls. I went to your place, and you weren't there. When are you going to return my money?"

I felt my cheeks burn with embarrassment. "I'll return it soon, sir," I mumbled.

"Soon? You've been saying that for two months!" His voice was loud, and people started staring. Chirag, who had been smiling moments ago, now looked furious.

Before things could escalate, I grabbed Chirag's hand to calm him down. I turned to Ramesh, trying to keep my voice steady. "Sir, please don't make a scene here."

"A scene? You think this is just a scene?" His voice was sharp, full of anger. "I'll teach you a lesson you won't forget. I want all my money back—now! Not just the EMI, but the entire amount!" Ramesh threatened, his voice rising.

Chirag stepped in. "Look, I don't know what's going on, but this is no way to speak to her."

Ramesh seemed to take a deep breath, then said with a sneer, "Listen, hero, tell your girlfriend if she doesn't return my money by Monday, she'll be in jail. I'll file a fraud case."

My heart sank. What was supposed to be a lovely evening with Chirag had turned into a disaster.

CHAPTER V

I was sitting on my bed, head down, feeling ashamed. Chirag stood in front of me, cautious and concerned. He wanted to know who Ramesh was and why he shouted at me. But I didn't want him to find out like this.

I couldn't bring myself to face him or even talk. After the incident at the restaurant, I left with tears in my eyes without saying a word. He followed, calling my name, but I didn't turn back.

As we walked toward our apartment, I stayed silent. I knew he cared; I could feel it, but I just couldn't speak.

Chirag came closer, knelt beside the bed, and gently touched my face, brushing a stray strand of hair away. His fingers on my skin made it impossible to hold back my tears any longer. I could see the pain in his eyes, and he wiped the tears from my cheeks.

Softly, he said, "Rishika, we are not just neighbors, we are friends. If you care for me, even just a little, please tell me who that guy at the restaurant was and what money he was talking about. I want to help."

I saw the sincerity in his eyes, and after taking a deep breath, I couldn't hide the truth anymore. "I came to this city from Delhi to chase my dreams. I wanted to start my own business, but I needed a loan to do that. I launched a few start-ups with borrowed money from various people. One of them was Ramesh Reddy—the man we met at the restaurant. I took a loan from him a couple of months ago for another start-up, but it failed. I'm struggling to repay not only his loan but others, too. That's why I started working at Zenith Networks. For a while, I managed to pay the EMIs, but…"

Should I tell him everything? No, I didn't want to add to his worries. I didn't want to tell him that Ramesh had made me a terrible offer. He said if I couldn't pay back the money I owed him, then I would have to become his mistress. He wanted me to stay at his farmhouse outside the city, entertain him and his friends on weekends, and be there for the rest of my life. When I refused, he became furious and demanded I repay the loan immediately.

He spoke to me in a calm, caring tone, "Rishika, it's great that you're independent and building a company, but the situation is serious now. I really think you should ask your family for help. I'm surprised you haven't told them about this yet, and why haven't they stepped in to support you?"

I forced a smile and said, "Family?" My voice cracked as I got emotional. "I don't have a family."

He looked confused. "What do you mean?"

"My parents passed away during the COVID-19 pandemic," I said, my voice trembling. Tears filled my eyes, blurring everything around me.

He became emotional, too. "My story is a lot like yours. I lost my parents in a car accident when I was a child. But you don't have to feel alone. No matter what, I'm here for you."

I didn't know much about him until then, but his words touched me deeply. Both of us began crying, remembering our parents and the loneliness we felt. Without saying a word, he gently hugged me.

I didn't resist – I needed that warmth. I could feel the strength in his arms, his muscles holding me close. After a few moments, we pulled away, and I saw something in his eyes – something I couldn't quite put into words.

"How much do you owe Ramesh Reddy?" he asked sharply.

"Why do you want to know?" I replied, unsure of his intentions.

"Just tell me the amount," he insisted.

Reluctantly, I said, "With interest, it's around twenty-five lakh rupees."

He paused for a moment, then spoke with calm confidence. "Don't worry. You rest now. Everything will be fine. Trust me."

Chirag leaned in and kissed my forehead as if he could somehow take all my problems away. His expression changed as if he had made up his mind about something, but I didn't know what. He left the flat, leaving me feeling confused and anxious.

I locked the door after he left.

I couldn't sleep; my mind was racing. I didn't hear the usual sound of the typewriter from his place, but I could smell the familiar scent of his Cuban cigar wafting in from the balcony.

Eventually, I fell asleep—though I don't know when. Maybe it was late into the night.

• • •

11th October, Sunday.

The sun rose, painting the sky red, its warm glow spilling right next to the balcony of my flat. A gentle breeze softly touched my skin, calming me. And there he was, standing right in front of me, smiling. For once, my heart felt light, with no weight of worry. It was like a dream. But wait— it wasn't a dream. It was real. I rubbed my eyes, trying to wake up properly. Damn! He was still there, standing in front of me.

"What the hell are you doing here?" I said, my voice rising in shock.

I quickly glanced down, checking if my clothes were decent. I was wearing a deep-neck top and shorts, and I couldn't help but wonder if his attention had been more on my cleavage than my face.

"Sorry, I just couldn't stop myself from coming over after last night. I wanted to check if you were okay," he said.

When he apologized, I could see the sincerity in his eyes.

"But how did you even get in? I remember locking the door when you left," I asked, still confused.

With a sly grin, he said, "I took your flat key last night before I left."

"What's the real reason you barged into my room?" I asked, a bit irritated. This wasn't the right way to visit a girl, especially when she's asleep—even if she does like you.

"I was worried about you," he said, standing up from the chair. "Black coffee?" he smiled again, and I couldn't help but smile back and nod.

I got up from bed and walked over to the balcony. The city was calm that Sunday morning and the roads were unusually peaceful. It was one of those rare days—no office, no rush to make tea or coffee. And when you have a thoughtful neighbor, the stress of morning tea disappears.

Chirag returned with two cups of black coffee. I took a sip, and the warm drink started to clear my mind. But with that clarity came the return of my worries. My smile faded as I remembered the looming problem with Reddy.

How was I going to repay the money by Monday?

"Don't worry. Everything will be fine," Chirag said softly, placing his hand on my shoulder.

Wait, did this guy just read my mind? He smiled knowingly and then said, "Forget about that jerk, Reddy. There's one thing he said that I kind of liked."

I frowned, confused. What could Reddy have possibly said that Chirag liked?

Chirag grinned. "Don't you remember? He called you my girlfriend."

I rolled my eyes and looked away, trying to stay focused. "That's not going to solve my problems," I muttered.

Chirag chuckled. "Your problems are already solved, dear! The money you owe Reddy? It's been taken care of."

"What?!" I nearly choked on my coffee, spilling it on my clothes in disbelief.

He smiled at me, doing his usual thing—casually brushing a stray lock of hair from his face. Then he walked into the room and opened my closet against the wall.

I was shocked and thought, *how dare he touch my closet?* Suddenly, I noticed a black backpack in his hand. Confused, I thought, *That's not mine. I didn't keep anything like that in my closet.*

Curious, I followed him into the room. The backpack looked heavy, and when he handed it to me, I opened it.

To my shock, it was full of money. I dropped it in surprise, but he quickly caught it and spread the money out on my bed like a blanket.

"What is this?" I asked, my voice shaky.

"Money, obviously, and in full amount which you owe Reddy," he chuckled. "Now, throw this in his face."

A hundred questions swirled in my mind.

"Is this yours?" I finally managed to ask.

"Not exactly, but it's yours now," he said, leaving me even more confused.

"Tell me, where did you get all this money?"

"Rishika, I've been in Mumbai for ten years. I've made a lot of connections. I got some help."

I couldn't believe what I was hearing. Just a few hours ago, I had told him about my problems, and now, somehow, he had all this money. *Did he sell a kidney or something?* I shook my head, dismissing the absurd thought.

"Chirag, I need to know – do you have connections to the underworld?"

He burst out laughing, but I was serious. "Tell me, I'm not joking."

"No, Rishika," he said, pausing for a moment. "I had a close friend in Mumbai. Together, we owned an ice cream shop. But I sold him my share. Now, take this money and give it to Ramesh Reddy. Let's end this for good."

"I can't take this money," I whispered.

"What did you say?"

"I can't take it."

"But why, Rishika? If you don't pay that scumbag, he'll have you thrown in jail! I don't want to see you in jail," he grabbed my shoulders, his voice full of emotion.

"This is your money, Chirag. I can't take it. You're my friend, but I don't want to be a burden to you."

His face fell. He stared out at the balcony for a couple of seconds before hurriedly scooping up the money from the bed as if it were trash.

"If you don't take it, I'll throw it all off the balcony!" he stammered.

With his hands full of money, he rushed toward the balcony. I ran after him and stood in front of him, blocking his way. He wouldn't look at me, his face clouded with emotion.

Without meeting my eyes, he said, "You think you're a burden to me, but you're not. You see me as just a friend, Rishika, but I have to tell you—you're so much more than that. You mean everything to me. You're my whole world. I wanted to say this with music and flowers, but... I LOVE YOU."

I stood there, stunned. I had a feeling, but hearing him say it so clearly left me speechless.

"Chirag, I... I like you too, and I really respect your feelings, but..."

"But what, Rishika? You have to take this money," Chirag said firmly.

I was torn. I needed to solve the problem with Ramesh Reddy, but I didn't want to accept Chirag's money.

"What are you thinking? Just take it," he insisted again.

Finally, I gave in and took the money.

Now, I could pay off everything I owed to Reddy and close that chapter for good. I couldn't express how grateful I was. With all that emotion, I gave Chirag a tight hug. He smiled, pulled me into his arms, and lifted me up in the air. I couldn't help but laugh—my happiness was written all over my face.

And this is how life is – when something good happens, something unexpected follows, too. I felt so happy and loved in Chirag's arms. I couldn't even remember the last time I felt this way. All my worries seemed to disappear. I was ready to pay off Ramesh, and that troubling chapter would be closed forever. I wouldn't have to see his face again.

That day, while I was lost in the joy of being with Chirag, I had no idea that there had been a robbery at CredZone last night.

CHAPTER VI

Chirag and I were having so much fun together. We danced, laughed, had a silly pillow fight, and did all sorts of goofy things. Then Chirag came up with a brilliant idea – he suggested we take a trip to Nandi Hills. I loved it immediately!

Nandi Hills is one of the best places in Bengaluru to enjoy nature, especially with someone you really like. So, of course, I agreed!

But here's the thing: if you live in Brookfield and want to catch the stunning sunset at Nandi Hills on the weekend, you've got to hurry. The place gets crowded fast, and everyone seems to have the same idea. We had to rush to get ready.

After about an hour, we were finally set to leave. Chirag stood at the front door, calling my name like mad. Just as I was about to walk out, my phone rang.

I glanced at the screen and saw the name—Dr. Neelam. Why was she calling me now?

"Hello, Doctor," I answered, trying to sound normal.

"Hello, Rishika. How are you? How are things going?" Dr. Neelam's voice was soft, the typical calming tone of a psychiatrist.

Meanwhile, Chirag was still calling from the door, probably thinking I was taking forever with makeup or something, but I had to deal with this.

"I'm fine, Doctor," I replied.

"Yes, I know you're fine. It was wonderful seeing you enjoying yourself yesterday," she said, sounding cheerful.

Wait, what? Yesterday? When did we meet? I had no memory of seeing her.

"When did you see me yesterday?" I asked, feeling puzzled as Chirag called my name again.

"At Cyrus's Corner. Our meeting was scheduled there," she replied.

Oh, I'd completely forgotten! Dr. Neelam was right; we had a meeting set at Cyrus' Corner.

"Sorry..." I apologized, feeling a bit embarrassed.

"Why are you apologizing? I should be sorry for being late," she said, then paused. "Rishika, I must say, you played the violin beautifully. I saw you, and I was so delighted by the tune."

Wait, what? She saw someone playing the violin, but that had been Chirag, not me. The place was crowded, and maybe, as an older lady, Dr Neelam hadn't noticed it was Chirag, not me, playing. But I decided to take the compliment mischievously. "Oh, thank you, Doctor," I said.

Chirag called my name again.

"I wanted to come over and tell you how beautifully you played," she continued. "But it was too crowded, so I couldn't get through."

Before she could finish, Chirag called my name yet again, so I quickly cut in, "Doctor, as you saw, I'm happy and doing well." I thought about telling her how someone had helped me find comfort and let go of my dark thoughts, but she was interrupted.

"But who was that man with you? He looked angry like he was shouting at you. What was going on?"

Oh no. She had seen Ramesh Reddy scolding me! I quickly reassured her, "Doctor, it was just a small misunderstanding. Don't worry, I'll handle it."

She tried to continue, but I interrupted, "Doctor, I have to go. I'm heading out on a picnic today. Thank you!" I hung up before she could say anything else.

Just then, Chirag walked into my room and, without a word, pulled me outside, eager to get our trip started.

Before heading to Nandi Hills in a rush, I had something really important to do.

I went to Ramesh Reddy's house to return all the money I owed him. I was informed that he was not at the house. He was out of the city or somewhere. Well, it was okay; I didn't have to see his face.

I returned the money to his faithful assistant and cleared my loan account with Reddy.

• • •

The morning air in Bengaluru was still crisp as Chirag and I set off from Brookfield, excited for our trip to Nandi Hills. Chirag had heard so much about the place, but this was his first time visiting.

Chirag was buzzing with energy, already planning every detail of our day together. He was always like that—full of ideas, spontaneous, and always pushing me to step outside my comfort zone. I admired that about him.

The drive took about an hour and a half, winding through the still sleepy outskirts of the city and climbing higher toward the hills. I found myself leaning back into my seat, enjoying the quiet moments when we weren't talking. It felt peaceful, like a world separate from the chaos of our regular lives.

As we got closer to the top, the landscape changed. Lush green trees lined the roads, and the sky opened up to reveal the soft glow of dawn. We arrived just as the sun was casting a golden light over the hilltop. Nandi Hills felt magical, almost otherworldly. The morning mist made everything seem ethereal. You could see the valley stretching far into the distance, covered in a soft, sleepy haze.

We made our way to one of the trails that led deeper into the hills. As we walked, I could feel the cool air on my skin and the soft rustle of leaves under our feet. Chirag kept cracking jokes, making me laugh so much that my cheeks hurt. We found a quiet spot under a large tree and sat there for a while, just taking it all in. I could see why this place was so popular—it was the perfect escape from the city's noise.

After a while, Chirag turned to me, his usual joking tone gone. He looked a little nervous, which was unusual for him. "Rishika," he said softly. He couldn't find the words to say to me; he just looked into my eyes.

At that moment, words didn't matter. It felt like our eyes were having a conversation all on their own. There was no need for words; we just understood each other's feelings. I liked Chirag too—so much. But this? This was new. I had never thought about us in that way, at least not seriously.

We spent the rest of the day exploring the hills, climbing rocks, taking silly selfies, and sharing snacks we had packed. The playful side of our friendship was still there, but now, there was something deeper between us. I could feel it, like a quiet hum in the background, something that made my heart race every time he smiled at me.

As the sun began to set, painting the sky with shades of pink and orange, we found ourselves standing at one of the lookout points. The view was breathtaking, but I barely noticed it. I was too focused on Chirag, who had moved closer to me. There was something in the air – an unspoken understanding. He leaned in, and so did I.

Our lips met softly, and at that moment, I knew. I had fallen in love with him. The worries, the doubts—they faded away as we shared our first kiss there, under the vast open sky of Nandi Hills. It felt right. It felt like home.

By the time we headed back down the hill, hand in hand, I realized that something had changed between us. It wasn't just friendship anymore—it was love. And I was ready for whatever came next.

What happened next was nothing short of a nightmare!

Throughout the day, I used my phone without bothering to charge it. By the time evening came, we were exhausted after our trip to Nandi Hills. We stopped at a café to grab something to eat. I realized my phone was dead, so I asked the friendly café staff if I could charge it at the counter. With a smile, he plugged it in for me.

As soon as I turned around, my phone started buzzing like crazy. Missed calls, messages—everything flooded in at once because my phone had died earlier. Curious, I picked it up to check the notifications.

My heart skipped a beat. There were endless missed calls and messages—all from Ramesh Reddy! A few were from others, but Ramesh had been bombarding my phone. Why was he calling me over and over? Was it just to thank me for clearing his entire loan in one night after that restaurant incident?

Before calling him back, I decided to read his messages. Some of them were strange: "Where are you? Call me back, where did you go? Don't make a fool of me!" I had no idea what was going on.

I tried to call him, but my phone died again. At that moment, Chirag walked over, reminding me that our coffee and food were getting cold. I decided to let it go for now. I left the phone charging and went back to the table with Chirag.

I had forgotten to call Reddy back. But honestly, who cares when you have a sweet and caring boyfriend who kisses away all your worries? When we got back to my flat late at night, nothing else seemed to matter. We had kissed passionately in the cab, not even bothering that the driver could see us in the rearview mirror. I felt more alive than ever before.

Now, we stood at the entrance of my flat. Our lips were saying goodbye, but our eyes and hearts had other plans. My heart raced, and I could feel the same energy in Chirag.

He smiled and said, "Alright then, goodbye, good night, sweet dreams." I couldn't speak, just opened the door and walked inside, leaving it open behind me.

I took a few steps into the living room when I suddenly felt his presence. Chirag rushed in, wrapping me in his arms from behind, his lips brushing my neck. My whole body shivered with excitement. I turned my face to meet his, and our lips connected again, this time even more intensely. Our tongues danced together as he lifted me into his strong arms, never breaking the kiss.

He carried me to my bedroom and gently laid me down on the bed as if I were something delicate.

We gazed into each other's eyes, knowing without words that there was no need to hold back anymore. He pulled off his polo shirt, revealing his toned, shirtless body. He looked so strong and handsome as he leaned over me. I could feel the warmth of his skin, and every part of me was drawn to him.

It was our first time together. The first time, we felt so close. Every part of him felt wonderful like he could keep my worries away. Chirag and I lay together under a single blanket, our arms wrapped around each other, with no clothes between us. He puffed on his cigar, and I could smell the smoky scent drifting around us. I wanted to try it too.

"May I?" I asked, pointing at the cigar.

He smiled and handed it over. Trying to look cool, I held it like a movie star, took a puff, and immediately started coughing. My face turned red as he burst out laughing. I gave him a stern look. "Don't tease me," I said.

After a while, I tried again, and this time, I didn't cough. We shared the cigar, watching the beautiful moon outside my window.

"Such a romantic moon tonight," he said, smiling.

"But I think your violin playing was even more romantic," I replied. "Will you teach me that tune?"

"Of course! Have you played before?"

"A long time ago, back in school."

"No problem, I'll show you," he said softly.

Just days ago, I was at my lowest, ready to give up on life. Now, I wanted to live—for moments like this, for him. The night felt endless as we gazed into each other's eyes, his arms around me, wrapped in warmth and peace.

CHAPTER VII

12th October, Monday.

Sundays are amazing, right? Whoever thought of Sunday was a genius. But the person who put Monday right after it? Oh, they must have been evil. I mean, seriously, who likes Mondays?

After a relaxing weekend, walking into the office feels like a tidal wave of tasks crashing down on you. There's suddenly so much work, and you wonder, "Did we commit a crime by enjoying our weekend?"

That Monday, I had a client meeting in the evening, which meant I had to work on a presentation. To make things worse, my team ran into a problem with a project. So, I had to sit down with them, figure out the issue, and try to fix it. Oh, and I also had to deal with HR because I skipped weekend training sessions. Who schedules those on weekends anyway? I hate that.

And then there's the social side of office life. You want to share stories from your weekend, right? I wanted to show some pictures and selfies from my trip out of town. And, of course, I couldn't wait to tell Sara about what happened with me and Chirag. We had a really exciting time, and I couldn't help but spill the details to her.

I remembered her reaction the first time I talked to her about Chirag in the office canteen. She looked annoyed and just walked away, leaving me there alone. But I really wanted to tell her about my weekend with Chirag, just to make her a bit jealous. I also wanted her to know I was in a relationship now, so if she had any feelings for me, she'd stop thinking about me that way.

Before I could even process what was happening, it felt like a bomb had dropped on my head. My phone rang—it was Ramesh Reddy. I picked up the call, and before I could even say 'hello,' he was shouting at me like a machine gun firing bullets.

"You cheated me! I'm Ramesh Reddy! Don't try to fool me, you bitch!"

I was stunned. "What the hell are you talking about?" I could only think of one thing—maybe the cash I gave him was fake, and that's why he was this angry.

"Did you really think I wouldn't find out about your little game?" he barked again.

"If you have something to say, say it clearly! I have no idea what you're accusing me of," my voice rose in frustration, but I didn't want to make a scene at the office. I stepped outside to the smoking area of the office where I could speak freely.

"Where did you get so much money overnight?" he demanded.

"That's none of your business," I shot back.

"Oh, it will be the police's business soon."

"What? Why?" Panic began to rise.

"I know where you got it. You robbed the CredZone and handed me the stolen money!"

CredZone—that name sounded familiar. Oh, yes, I remembered now! It was the loan company's office near my apartment. I had seen Chirag standing there in front of it late on Friday night.

How could Dinesh accuse me of robbing that company?

"What? Are you insane? Are you out of your mind?"

"You think I'm joking? Just wait until I tell the police your name and give them this money."

"Hold on, I don't even know what you're talking about! I didn't even know there was a robbery at CredZone!"

"Stop playing dumb! Watch the news. The robbery happened on Saturday night, and you gave me all that money on Sunday morning!"

"You're crazy! I got the money from a friend. I didn't rob!"

There was a brief pause before he said, "Then your friend did."

The call ended abruptly. I stood there in shock, my body trembling, unsure of what to do next. First, I had to check the news that Ramesh mentioned. I opened the news app on my phone.

A reporter was shouting, *"This is huge breaking news from Bengaluru! Police are still searching for clues to catch the thief who robbed CredZone, a lending company. The robbery happened late Saturday night. The thief shot and badly injured all four security guards before breaking into the office. He stole around twenty lakh rupees in cash from the safe. CCTV footage shows him wearing a black hoodie and a black mask.*

Police sources say the robbery was carefully planned. CredZone's office is in a deserted area with no public around at night. Meanwhile, opposition leaders are condemning the incident, questioning the city's law and order."

I was sitting at my desk, my eyes glued to my phone screen as I watched the news. My heart was racing, almost as if I were the one who committed the robbery. Just then, Sara startled me from behind.

"Hey, why are you looking at this old news? Didn't you see it yesterday?"

"No," I replied, still focused on finding more details about the robbery. I wanted to know if the robber's face was caught on any CCTV, but I couldn't find anything. I was also annoyed by what Ramesh Reddy had said on the phone call.

Sara's voice pulled me out of my thoughts. "Oh, I remember! You were out yesterday at Nandi Hills, enjoying nature. So, what happened there? You promised to show me the pictures from your trip. Show me, Yaar!"

I wasn't in the mood to chat with Sara or share the photos. My eyes stayed on the phone, trying to find more updates on the robbery.

Sara then joked, "Has your neighbor—what's his name? Oh yeah, Chirag—stolen the cash from that office?"

Her words made my blood boil. My face flushed with anger, and without saying a word, I stood up and walked out.

I had a meeting with some juniors who were stuck with a tech problem, and I needed to help them find a solution. I could hear Sara calling my name and apologizing, but I ignored her.

Sara had crossed the line. She was accusing Chirag of being a robber, all because I had spent some time with him. Maybe Sara was just jealous, thinking I had something going on with Chirag. But her comments were out of line.

What really bothered me was something else—the CredZone had been robbed. I remembered that day so clearly. Chirag had told me about the incident, describing it as part of his own storyline. He said his hero would come in, holding a pistol and rob the office.

Later, as we were walking back from Cyrus' Corner to our flats, still embarrassed after the awkward moment with Ramesh Reddy, I noticed Chirag standing on the road, staring at the CredZone office. His gaze was intense, filled with a strange curiosity. It felt like he knew something I didn't, something he wasn't telling me, but I couldn't figure out what.

Ramesh had hinted that my friend might be behind the robbery, and that thought made me uneasy. I had to talk to Chirag to find out the truth. So, I called him, but his phone was switched off. I called again, but still, nothing.

I wanted to scream—just to release the tension building inside me. So, I did. The meeting with my juniors was in the office conference room. I let all my anger out on them.

"You guys are hopeless!" I yelled at my juniors. "You're all computer science engineers, but you have no common sense! You can't even visualize things properly. You're so unfocused on the problems, the project, and what the clients need!"

I wasn't sure if I was just frustrated or if they had really messed up this time. My anger had already been building after that stressful phone call with Reddy. On top of that, I still hadn't gotten any answers from Sara about why she was calling Chirag a thief. I tried reaching out to Chirag, too, but his phone was off both times I called.

Had he done something terrible? Did he actually steal the cash from the CredZone? Was he really a thief? The questions kept spinning in my mind, and I felt completely lost.

My phone buzzed—it was Chirag. My heart raced when I saw his name flash on the screen. But before answering, I snapped at the team one last time, "You have one hour to clean up your mess. Don't come back without a solution for the project."

They scattered like prisoners running from their jailor. After making sure the conference room was empty, I finally picked up the call. "Chirag, where have you been?"

"Darling, that's no way to greet me," he teased. "No 'hi,' no 'hello,' just 'where are you?' You must've missed me." He sounded casual, but I wasn't in the mood for sweet talk.

"Where were you?" I asked again, my tone serious this time.

Sensing the shift, he replied more sincerely, "I'm at home."

"What were you doing?"

"I was trying to write for my novel. Actually, after last night's... romance, I've been inspired to—"

I cut him off, not wanting to relive last night's intimate details. "Why was your phone switched off?"

"Yaar, I needed some peace. I turn off my phone when I'm writing."

"Do you know how many times I called you?"

"Yeah, I saw the seven missed calls as soon as I turned my phone back on. That's why I called you right away. Why are you grilling me like a CID officer?"

"Where did you get the money you gave me?" My voice was sharp, and I wanted the truth.

Chirag hesitated. "Rishika... why are you asking? Is something wrong with the money?"

"Just tell me the truth."

"The truth is—" Before he could finish, a colleague burst into the room. "Our client is here. The meeting's about to start in Mr

Deshmukh's office."

"Just give me two minutes," I said, waving them off. Turning my attention back to the call, I pressed Chirag again. "Yes, what were you saying?"

"Rishika, you've got a meeting. Go attend it. We'll talk later."

"Don't worry about the meeting," I snapped. "I can handle it. Just answer my question."

Chirag sighed. "The money came from my Mumbai source. I told you that already. What's going on?"

"You gave me the money on Sunday morning, right?"

"Yeah, Sunday morning."

"Late Saturday night, a lending company's office near us was robbed. It was the same office you mentioned while standing in front of it on Friday evening."

"I just heard about that... wait, Rishika, are you saying—" His voice grew anxious. After a pause, he continued, "Rishika, my dear, what are you implying? Do you think I stole that money? That I'm a thief? Do you really not trust me? You think I robbed the cash and gave you stolen money? Am I that kind of person?"

I wasn't in the mood to listen to him. I interrupted and said, "Tell me, why were you standing at the CredZone that night when we were coming back from Cyrus' Corner? I saw you looking at it strangely. It was Saturday night, the same night the robbery happened a few hours later. I found you standing right in front of that. Don't lie to me—I saw you."

His voice shook as he answered, "Yes, I was right there in front of CredZone. As I said, I was only there to get ideas for my novel. The main character in my story robbed a shop, so I needed to see what the place looked and felt like. I just wanted my writing to feel real. That's all; that's why I was there."

Hearing this, I was stunned. I felt an emotional shock and a deep sense of guilt. His voice softened, and I could tell he was hurt. Was he crying?

I felt awful. What was wrong with me? He was helping me, and I treated him like a criminal. And all because Reddy had put this nonsense in my head. I was mad at myself. I spoke softly, "Chirag... baby, are you crying? Please don't cry. I didn't mean—"

"Just tell me how you came to this conclusion. Someone must've messed with your mind for you to think this way."

I couldn't bring myself to tell him that Ramesh had poisoned my thoughts. "Listen," I said, "I need to go to the meeting now. We'll talk later, over your favorite ginger-mint black coffee, at my flat. Okay? Don't worry about the nonsense I just said."

"Okay," he replied, and I hung up. My heart felt lighter after talking to him, and I was ready to focus on impressing our potential client.

It was 7:30 p.m., and I was finally getting ready to leave the office. The client meeting had gone on much longer than expected, but overall, it went well. The client had sent his younger brother, a guy in his early twenties, to represent him.

He was polite and really easy to work with. He understood everything we discussed—probably because he was a techie, too, with a degree in computer science. Compared to the usual client, a grumpy man in his fifties who constantly complained and compared us to big companies in the city, this was a breeze.

As I walked toward the main door to punch out, Sara appeared behind me, her face lit up with a smile and an apologetic "sorry" on her lips. Sara, a sweet, chubby girl, always looked so adorable when she apologized that no one could stay mad at her. I waved off her "sorry" and playfully pulled her cheeks. We both punched our cards and headed out together.

While we waited for the elevator, Sara beamed and said, "You did an amazing job!"

"Huh? What do you mean?"

"In the meeting, you totally nailed it and convinced the client!"

I laughed. "Yeah, well, he was a nice guy, easy to convince."

Sara shot me a mischievous glance and jokingly said, "It wasn't just your words. Your cleavage did half the job! The guy couldn't stop staring."

I playfully smacked her. Sara had a habit of making these silly, teasing remarks. Luckily, the elevator arrived before anyone overheard us.

As we stepped in, Sara grinned and asked, "By the way, where's the photo?"

"Photo? What photo?"

"From your Nandi Hills trip yesterday! Show me!"

You know that proud feeling when your friend, who's also a girl, asks to see photos of your trip with your cute boyfriend? That's exactly how I felt.

My chest puffed up with excitement. But then, panic set in—where were the photos with Chirag?

As I scrolled through my phone, I realized something strange. All the pictures were of me—no Chirag anywhere! What was going on? I remember taking tons of selfies with him at every scenic spot. Yet, when I looked, only my photos showed up.

Before I could figure it out, Sara grabbed my phone and started scrolling. I was anxious. "Wow, Rishika, you look so hot against that Nandi Hills backdrop," she said. We stepped out of the lift, and I said, "But I didn't know where Chirag's photo had gone?"

She jokingly said, "You would forget to take his pictures and just focus on yourself."

I replied, a bit irritated, "I took his photos, too! I just don't know where they went."

Sara laughed. "Oh, so your neighbor-turned-boyfriend's photos just disappeared? Is he a ghost or something?"

Her words stung. Sara always made these kinds of jokes about Chirag. I thought she was my best friend, but sometimes she could be so hurtful.

Frustrated, I snatched my phone back and searched again. And there they were! All the pictures of Chirag and me are right in front of me. Maybe I'd saved them in a different folder or something—smartphones can be weird like that.

Triumphantly, I shoved the phone in front of Sara's face. "See? Here's Chirag, you jealous witch! You always act like you're better than me, but look—Chirag is real and in these photos!"

Sara's face went pale. She looked uncomfortable as she scrolled through the photos. I could tell she was burning with jealousy. I felt a surge of satisfaction seeing her like that. She handed the phone back to me, clearly shaken.

"What's wrong?" I called out as she started to walk away. "Don't you have anything to say about Chirag and me? How do we look as a couple?"

She turned around, visibly nervous. "You both look good together, just like you said," she mumbled before hurrying off.

Suddenly, Sara turned back and said, "Rishika, Dr. Neelam called. She said you missed your session. You should go—it might help."

I brushed off her comment and watched as she walked away.

CHAPTER VIII

When I walked into my flat around 9 p.m., I immediately noticed two things. First, the familiar scent of a cigar, and second, a deep, romantic tune from a violin that both calmed and excited me. I moved forward and saw Chirag sitting near the balcony in one of those old chairs my landlord had given me.

His eyes were closed, but he was smiling, completely lost in the beautiful melody he was playing. It was the same tune he played at Cyrus's Corner that night, which was supposed to be our first date—until Ramesh Reddy ruined it. Ugh, I didn't want to think about that idiot tonight.

I tossed my handbag aside and fell onto the bed, closing my eyes and letting the sound of Chirag's violin carry me away. I felt like I was in another world. But then his voice brought me back to reality: "Coffee's ready, ma'am," he said with a playful bow, like a waiter in a hotel.

I laughed and headed to the kitchen. He kept playing as I came back with two mugs of black coffee and some sandwiches. He'd made them for me. Husband material, right? He didn't just make coffee; he made sandwiches, too. What was I even thinking? We were already so close. It didn't make sense for us to keep paying rent for two separate flats. We should have just moved in together.

I sat down next to him, feeling the soft breeze from the balcony. It touched my face and played with my hair as I sipped my coffee, listened to the violin, and bit into the sandwich. What more could I want from life? After a long day of dealing with tech and code, this was the perfect way to spend an evening.

I leaned in and gave him a soft, slow kiss. It was his reward for everything—for the coffee, the sandwich, and the beautiful music. When I pulled back, he looked straight into my eyes and kissed me in return, a deep, passionate kiss. He was good—better than any guy I had kissed before.

"How's the coffee?" he asked, gently rubbing my head to ease the headache and stress from work. He sat on the chair while I was on the floor, making sure his hands massaged my head just right.

"It's amazing! And before you ask about the sandwich, it's delicious too," I said, grabbing the last piece. "I have to say, you're a great chef. A violinist, a writer, a shooter, and now a chef too—so many talents."

"You forgot one more thing," he said with a smile.

"What?" I asked, curious.

"Your lover—I'm your lover too. And I think that should be the number one thing on the list."

I laughed and hugged him, playfully spitting a bit of sandwich onto his gray sleeveless T-shirt like a child.

I said with deep regret, "I thought you would be upset with me for how I behaved and the way I questioned you at the office."

He smiled and gently replied, "Oh no, dear, upset with you? Never. I could never be angry with you."

Just then, I noticed something new on my balcony. It was an areca palm plant. Excitedly, I asked, "Hey, what's that? Did you plant an areca palm on my balcony?"

He nodded and said, "Yes, dear. Your balcony looked empty, with no plants. So, I thought I'd add one for you. This plant will remind you of me when I'm not around. Plants make us happy, you know."

I walked over to the balcony, touched the soft leaves, and smiled. It felt nice to see something green and alive - who doesn't love that feeling?

Suddenly, I remembered something.

"Wait, let me tell you something. I always forget, but this time, I remembered!" Returning back from the balcony to the room, I said.

"Yeah? Go ahead," he encouraged.

"I want to learn that violin tune from you. I've been dying to learn it."

"Why? I'm always here to play it for you whenever you want."

"That's nice, but I want to be the one to play it for you. No arguments, just teach me," I insisted.

"Alright," he said, handing me the violin, "Just hold it and let's start."

Learning to play a romantic, emotional violin tune from my loving boyfriend felt like one of those sweet moments shared between couples. It was the first time I was trying to learn the tune, and back then, I didn't know that it would be the last special memory we'd have together.

I held the violin in my hands, and he stood behind me, showing me how to use the strings. As he moved closer, I turned around and looked into his brown eyes. At that moment, I couldn't help but melt, and soon our lips met. But then, I remembered why I was there—to learn the violin—so I quickly returned to practicing.

Again, he was behind me, guiding me with instructions on how to tune the strings. But every time I felt his breath on my neck, his warmth, I would turn, and we would kiss again. This happened over and over.

I was supposed to learn the violin, but instead, we kept falling into these romantic moments. We kissed, we played, we danced, and even fought. At one point, I got mad at him for not teaching me the violin properly.

Time just flew by, filled with joy and carefree laughter.

But as one of my old school teachers used to say, "The more you laugh, the more you cry." I realized that evening, just like in my school days, that happiness always seemed to be followed by sadness. And this time, the sadness came with a call—from Reddy.

I picked up the phone, but I didn't say a word. On the other side, he spoke first. His voice was slurred like he had been drinking. "Hello, dear dacoit, bandit queen. Have you chosen a name that fits your profession of stealing money from others?" He then burst into laughter, a sound that felt like it was drilling into my ears.

I glanced at the clock – it was 12:30 a.m. "Is this really the time for you to call me?" I asked, trying to stay calm.

"But this is your time, isn't it?" he sneered. "The time when you break into others' safes and rob them." He laughed again, louder this time.

I stayed as calm as I could. "Listen, Mr. Reddy, you're clearly drunk. I don't want to talk to you right now. We'll talk later."

Before I answered the call, Chirag had warned me not to pick up. He could sense trouble, but I wanted to know what was going on in Ramesh's head. Now, as I listened to the conversation, I could feel Chirag's anger. He was watching me closely, furious at what I was going through. He even tried to take the phone from me, but I held on.

Reddy, however, had lost it. He yelled through the phone, "You bitch! You don't want to talk to me? I'll show you what I can do!"

"Stop talking like this! What do you want from me? I gave you all your money!" My voice shook as I cried and screamed.

Chirag stood beside me, his eyes full of anger toward Reddy but with love and care for me. He gently patted my shoulder.

"Money... You gave me money, and now I want something else," Reddy said, laughing like a madman. "You know what I mean." His laughter echoed in my mind.

"What are you talking about?"

"Just say yes to my offer," he whispered with a hint of lust in his voice over the phone. "Come to my farmhouse; stay with me forever, my darling. I'll clear all your debts. I'll forgive everything you've done. Just come to me, baby."

"Stop talking nonsense!" I yelled, feeling humiliated. Tears streamed down my face, but I stood firm. I asked one last time, trying to stay calm. "I didn't rob anyone. My friend helped me pay off your loan."

"Fine, if you don't accept my offer, I'll go to the police and tell them everything. The police are hunting for the robber, and they'll take you and your friend. You'll end up behind bars, and who knows what they'll do to you." With that, he hung up the phone.

His words swirled in my mind, leaving me confused and scared.

Chirag pulled me into a hug. "Don't worry about what he said," he whispered.

"He said he'll go to the police and accuse us of being robbers if we don't give him the money," I said through my sobs.

Chirag's face darkened with anger. "He's crazy. Let him go to the police. When they come, I'll tell them I gave you the money. They'll have to question me, not you. Don't worry."

"But Chirag," I said, trembling. "You don't know his connections. He could frame us. The police are desperate to catch the robbers. If Ramesh hands me over to them, they won't hesitate to lock me up to shut the media up."

Chirag was about to say something, but I waved him off. With tears in my eyes, I looked at Chirag and said, "Reddy made me an offer. He said if I moved to his farmhouse and stayed there as his mistress, he wouldn't go to the police."

"What?" Chirag's anger boiled over. "You should have told me this first!" He gently sat me down on the bed, then stormed toward the door.

"Chirag, where are you going?" I called after him.

"I'm going to kill that bastard," he yelled.

I rushed after him, grabbing his arm. "No, Chirag. He's not worth it. He's just trying to dump his garbage on us. Don't sink to his level."

"Don't stop me, Rishika! I'll teach him a lesson."

"You're angry right now. You're not thinking straight. Take a deep breath..."

"How can you expect me to stay calm when he abused you?" Chirag's voice trembled with rage. "I should break his neck!"

"Chirag, let it go," I held his hand as he reached the main door, about to leave.

His eyes were burning with fury. "I love you, Rishika. I won't let anyone hurt you. I can't just sit here and do nothing."

Tears welled up in my eyes. "Okay, go... but promise me you won't do anything reckless. Just talk to him, make him understand. Promise me."

"I promise," he said, kissing my forehead before walking out the door.

As I watched him leave, my heart ached with worry. I knew he cared for me deeply, but I couldn't shake the fear that something might go wrong.

Only ten minutes had passed since Chirag left, but I was already restless.

Waiting for something important can feel like the hardest thing. It's like a pregnant woman who loves her unborn child so much that she can't wait to see its face, but still, she has to wait. Or like a farmer who waters his plants and eagerly waits for fruits, knowing he must be patient. Even a prisoner waits for the day his time will be over, but he knows that day will come eventually. Waiting for answers when you desperately want them feels endless.

I knew the journey from my flat to Ramesh Reddy's house would take Chirag about half an hour each way, and convincing him would take time, too. So, I figured Chirag wouldn't return for at least an hour and a half after he left. But I was eager to know what was happening between them at his house.

My mind started racing with terrible thoughts. What if Ramesh, who was like a villain from a Hindi movie, tried to hurt Chirag, the hero of my life? I swore to myself that if Ramesh harmed him, I would take revenge with my own hands.

But then I worried—Chirag had been so angry when he left; what if he hurt Reddy instead? Could he have broken Ramesh's neck or paralyzed him for life? What if the police caught Chirag and put him in jail? I couldn't imagine my life without him. My mind was spinning like a rollercoaster, and I developed a terrible headache.

Just when I thought I couldn't take it anymore, I heard Chirag's footsteps outside my flat. I rushed to the door like a bird flying to its nest. He looked calm, more content than I had ever seen him.

"What happened there?" I asked, breathless.

"Nothing, sweetheart," he said, pulling me into his arms. He carried me to my room and sat down on the chair by the balcony, placing me on his lap. He gently ran his fingers through my hair.

"What about your headache?" he asked.

"Shoot the headache! Just tell me everything that happened," I demanded.

He smiled mischievously. "Nothing bad happened. Your Ramesh Reddy is fine."

I didn't appreciate his teasing. With a fake frown, I raised my hand as if to hit him. He laughed and brushed a strand of hair off his face.

"Details?" I insisted. I needed to know everything—how my Chirag handled that brat.

"I first told him where I got the money that I gave you. I called a friend in Mumbai who arranged the money for me against my share in the ice cream parlor business. Ramesh spoke to him, and after a conversation, he realized the truth."

"And then?" I asked eagerly.

"Then he was ashamed. You should've seen his face! He wanted to call and apologize to you, but I told him not to. I said I didn't want him bothering you anymore. But to prove his regret, I made him record an apology video for you," Chirag said, his eyes full of respect and love.

"What? Did he make an apology video for me? That's amazing! Show me!" I screamed in excitement.

Chirag took out his phone and showed me the video. On the screen, Ramesh looked pale, with a bruise under his left eye.

In the video, he said, *"Rishika, I'm sorry. I shouldn't have treated you that way. You've returned all the money I owed, and I don't need anything more from you. I'm truly sorry."*

I couldn't contain my happiness. It felt like I had won an Olympic medal.

I hugged Chirag tightly. "Oh my God, Chirag, you've done something incredible for me!" I said, beaming. "But tell me one thing—what happened to his face? He looked like he'd been beaten up."

Chirag turned his face away, avoiding my eyes. I gently turned his head back toward me. "What happened?"

"Rishika, do you really think I'd let him go so easily after what he did to you?" he said, his voice full of anger.

"Did you beat him up?" I asked anxiously. "Yes, I did. I won't lie to you. He deserved it," Chirag admitted, looking emotional. I felt proud of my strong and loving partner.

I kissed him and said, "You did the right thing. That guy deserved it."

• • •

The next morning, a shocking headline appeared in the newspaper:

Dinesh Thakur, Senior Banker, Shot Dead!

CHAPTER IX

13th, Tuesday.

I could feel it from the start of the day—Sara was avoiding me. Since morning, she hasn't spoken to me the way she usually does. After joining work, we all had to attend a meeting led by our team leader. Everyone was gathered, and Sara made eye contact with all of us, but she ignored me, acting like I wasn't even in the room. I noticed it clearly.

During the meeting, one of my colleagues, J.K., a bald guy known for his cheeky, sometimes inappropriate jokes, cracked a non-veg joke. Everyone laughed, and Sara joined in. But when I made a joke a little later, everyone laughed except for her. It became clear to me—it had to be because of what happened between us yesterday.

I didn't let it bother me. She wasn't the center of my world, after all. Why should I care? I even tried to make things normal by asking her out for coffee after the meeting. But she declined with a formal smile. At that moment, it became obvious—she was jealous.

I was now in a relationship with a guy, and I had broken her dream. She had wanted something more from me, something I could never give—she had imagined a romantic relationship between us. It made me uncomfortable just thinking about it.

She had been upset with me since last night, and I realized it the moment my phone buzzed and Dr Neelam's name flashed on the screen. Remember that one classmate from school who would always tell the teacher everything, even your secrets, and then you'd get in trouble? Well, Sara, my so-called best friend, was like that classmate, and Dr Neelam was the teacher.

Without much enthusiasm, I picked up the call. "Hello, Doctor," I said.

"Hello, Rishika. How are you doing?" Dr Neelam's voice had that typical psychiatrist tone, like she thought I was crazy.

"I'm good, Doctor."

Then, in her usual calm voice, she said, "I know. Sara told me last night that you've found someone—your boyfriend, your special one." See? Just like back in school, Sara had spilled everything to the "teacher."

"Yes, Doctor. I'm lucky to have found him."

"And may I know the name of this lucky man who stole your heart?" she asked.

"His name is Chirag," I replied.

"Oh, nice name! When will you introduce me to him?" Dr. Neelam inquired as if it were the most normal thing in the world.

Wait, what? Why would I introduce my psychiatrist to my boyfriend? Have you ever heard of someone doing that? It sounded absurd. I thought, "Isn't it weird to introduce your shrink to your boyfriend?"

"I don't have any plans for that," I said, trying to keep my cool.

"I understand, Rishika. It's not easy, right? It's embarrassing to introduce your psychiatrist to your boyfriend."

She got that part, at least. But then she said, "You can introduce me as your aunt. I won't say anything bad about you."

What? Now, she was getting on my nerves.

"I'm not sure, Doctor. Besides, Chirag might not want to meet my aunt just yet. It's still early in our relationship," I replied, hoping she'd drop the subject.

"Just a casual meeting, Rishika. Do this for me," she insisted. I couldn't understand why she was so persistent. She continued, "Think about it and let's meet Chirag this weekend."

She hung up, and I felt like I had just agreed to introduce Chirag to my grandmother.

Later, I was about to take a break for lunch after working non-stop for three hours. There was so much to do, and I hadn't even had a chance to message Chirag. Breakfast had been delicious, but I hadn't been able to tell him because I'd eaten it quickly in the office cab.

I headed to the canteen without bothering to ask Sara to join me, which was unusual. On any other day, we would have gone together, arm in arm. But not today.

Just as I was about to leave, a peon came to my desk and said, "Ma'am, there's a police inspector waiting for you in the conference room."

"What? Who?" I asked, stunned.

"The police inspector is waiting for you," he repeated.

I was shocked. Why would the police be here, and why would an inspector want to talk to me? Feeling confused, I walked toward the conference room. As I passed by, it felt like the entire office was staring at me, like I was some kind of rare creature.

I glanced at Sara, who stood by her desk, watching me. Was she enjoying the fact that I had to go to the police for questioning? Had Sara planned all of this?

When I entered the conference room, I noticed the large LED TV was on. But before I could focus on the policemen, my eyes froze on the news flashing across the screen.

"Ramesh Reddy, a banker in his early fifties, was shot dead late last night. Police are searching for the killer."

I was in shock. I couldn't believe what I was seeing on TV. I sank into a chair, my eyes still glued to the screen.

The news showed Ramesh's body at the crime scene, but the blood and his face were blurred out. A warning flashed, saying, "These images may be disturbing." Suddenly, the TV went black. That's when I finally noticed the two policemen standing in the room.

One was Sub-Inspector Vijay Reddy, dark-skinned with sharp black eyes, smiling as he held the remote. The other, a constable named Sharma, was older, with a potbelly and a look that suggested he might burst into laughter at any moment.

SI Reddy spoke first. "From the way you just saw TV news, two things are clear. One, you knew Mr. Ramesh Reddy. And two, before entering this room, you didn't know that he was shot at close range with a 9mm pistol."

Just like you, I also thought about Chirag. Did Chirag do this? Did he kill Ramesh, as he hinted when he left the flat last night? No, he probably wouldn't do that. He had already told me what happened there. But he still went to his house late last night. Did the police know about it?

"Mmm...yeah, I know him," I said, my voice trembling. I had never been questioned by the police before, and I could feel my heart racing. The fact that they were here meant they had some clue about what happened last night. Chirag, what did you do, baby?

The inspector's thick black eyebrows arched as he studied me. He wanted more information, so I continued, "I know him. He invested in one of my start-ups."

"You mean, he gave you a loan?" the inspector clarified.

"Yes," I nodded.

"And you repaid him?"

"Yes," I replied quickly, praying he wouldn't ask how much money I had borrowed or how I managed to pay it back. Those questions would open up a lot of things I couldn't explain.

"Then why did he call you late last night?" His voice sounded thoughtful as if he was asking himself more than me.

I knew things were getting complicated. I had to be careful with my words. I wasn't about to tell the police that Ramesh suspected I repaid him by robbing the CredZone's safe. The inspector interrupted my thoughts.

"Miss Rishika, you do know that you were the last person Mr Reddy spoke to before he was shot dead. That's why we're here. So, tell me, why did he call you at 12:30 at night?"

Taking a deep breath, I lied, "Sir, I had been asking him to invest in another one of my start-ups. Last night, he called me at the time you mentioned, saying he was finally ready to invest."

"At that time late at night, did he decide to tell you he was ready to invest?" The inspector raised an eyebrow.

"Yes, sir," I said, trying to sound calm.

"Don't you think that's an odd time for such news?"

"Yes, sir, I know. It seemed from his voice that he was drunk. I told him we could talk later, but he insisted on discussing it right then. You know how it is, sir. Sometimes, to get an investor for a start-up, we have to put up with things like that."

"Did he say anything else to you?" the inspector asked.

I hesitated. Ramesh had accused me over the phone, yelling that I'd robbed to pay him back. But I wasn't about to tell the inspector that. Instead, I shook my head. "No, sir."

"Did he seem in danger? Was he acting normal?" he asked.

I paused for a moment before answering, "Yes, sir. Ramesh was just being himself. Nothing seemed unusual."

The inspector exchanged a glance with Constable Sharma and then, out of nowhere, he showed me something on his phone screen. My stomach churned. My knees felt weak. I rushed out of the room, heading straight for the washroom.

I vomited into the sink again and again. The image on the inspector's phone flashed in my mind—it was Ramesh Reddy, dead. He had been shot in the forehead, right between his eyes. His face was unrecognizable, smashed, blood everywhere, the floor covered in it. I had never seen anything so horrifying in my life. I vomited once more.

Suddenly, I felt a soft hand gently patting my shoulder and back. I lifted my face from the sink and looked into the mirror. Sara's reflection stared back at me. Was she here to mock me, to enjoy my misery? No, her eyes told a different story. She looked concerned. Her gentle pats on my shoulder were calming, and I realized I needed this comfort.

It seemed as if my pain affected her, too. After washing my face, without thinking, I turned around and hugged her. To my surprise, she hugged me back, arms wide open. At that moment, all my bitterness toward her faded. I just needed someone to hold me, and I began crying softly on her shoulder. I didn't know if I was crying over Chirag, missing Sara, or the horrifying image I saw on the police phone. But Sara stayed with me, calming me down.

After a while, Sara led me out of the washroom, holding my hand like a mother. We walked into the conference room, where Sub-Inspector Vijay and Constable Sharma were waiting. Without hesitation, Sara addressed SI Vijay, her voice firm, "Don't you think a lady constable should be present while questioning her?"

Vijay cleared his throat, clearly taken aback by her words. "We weren't interrogating Miss Rishika. It was just a routine inquiry. She was the last person Ramesh Reddy spoke to before he was shot. Everything was normal."

Sara, not backing down, replied, "Normal? Then why did she run to vomit? She's clearly shaken."

The inspector looked irritated. "I only showed her the last picture of Ramesh Reddy. Maybe that scared her."

"Why would you do that? Why show such a horrifying image?" Sara pressed.

"I wanted to see her reaction when she saw the body," he responded.

"And why exactly?" Sara asked, almost as if she were interrogating him.

"Why should I explain myself to you? Are you her lawyer?" SI Vijay's voice rose.

"I'm not, but my father is her lawyer—Mr. Virendra Rao. Ever heard of him? Or should I call the commissioner? He's a close friend of my father," Sara said confidently.

How could I forget Sara's father was a renowned lawyer with powerful connections? The look on the policemen's faces said it all. SI Vijay's expression shifted. "No need to trouble the commissioner, ma'am," he said, quickly adding, "I needed to check her reaction to see if she was involved in Ramesh's murder."

What? The policeman thought I had killed Reddy. But why?

Sara, equally shocked, asked, "Why would you suspect Rishika?"

"We have to suspect everyone. It's how we work," SI Vijay replied.

"And what did you conclude from her reaction?" Sara asked, her tone sharp.

"From her reaction, it seems she didn't kill Ramesh."

Sara chuckled. "So that's your method? Showing a body to gauge reactions? What if she had stayed calm—would you have arrested her based on that?"

SI Vijay didn't answer. He glanced at Constable Sharma, and they seemed ready to leave. Before leaving, Vijay turned on the TV with the remote.

On the news channel, ACP Arjun Shetty was addressing reporters outside the police commissioner's office. He looked slightly annoyed but spoke calmly.

"Our investigations are ongoing. We will catch the criminal soon. We have CCTV footage from Ramesh Reddy's house, and we believe the person in the footage could be the killer. Before his death, Ramesh called the police and mentioned he had information about the robber who looted CredZone. We suspect this is why he was murdered. The

CCTV footage shows a person entering his house, and we identified this person as the same one who robbed the lending company's office—same height, same gestures."

As soon as the footage appeared on the screen, my heart pounded. My body broke into a cold sweat, and I nearly screamed. The person in the footage wasn't clear, but I recognized the black hoodie. It was Chirag.

CHAPTER X

Sara spoke like she was a CID inspector. 'The guy was smart. He hid his face with a hoodie and cap so the CCTV couldn't recognize him.' She sounded so sure, maybe because she was the daughter of a criminal lawyer.

We were sitting in the canteen for lunch, but the lunch hour had passed while the police questioned me. I had no appetite. I'd vomited so much that I couldn't taste anything, and honestly, I didn't even want to come here. But Sara insisted.

All I wanted was to go to bed and cry. Cry over what Chirag had done. I trusted him so much, but everything was shattered. The news made it clear—the guy who murdered Ramesh Reddy was also involved in the robbery. That meant everything Chirag told me was a lie. The money he gave me to pay off Reddy's loan came from the robbery. I believed him without a doubt. Was I a fool?

Sara waved a burger in front of me, her loud voice pulling me back to reality. 'What's wrong? Why are you thinking such weird stuff?'

'Nothing,' I replied, hesitating. How could I tell her that my boyfriend, Chirag, was a liar and a cheat? Instead, I said, 'I'm not hungry. The smell of the food is enough to make me full.'

'Oh, that's why you're so slim,' Sara joked with her usual playful grin. 'You just sniff food, and you're full. I, on the other hand, have to actually eat!' She laughed, and somehow, despite everything, she made me smile too. Sara was so good, and Chirag... he was so cruel.'

"Rishika, can I ask you something? Of course, only if you don't mind," Sara said. "As far as I know, Ramesh Reddy was the financier for one of your start-ups, right?"

"Yeah, that's true," I replied.

"Well, it's better that he's dead now. You don't have to worry about paying back his loan."

"But I already paid it off," I said calmly.

"What?!" Sara's eyes widened in shock. The piece of burger she was eating fell from her mouth, and I bit my tongue, realizing I shouldn't have said that. Now, she was going to ask how I managed to pay the whole loan.

"How did you pay off the entire loan?" she asked, just as I feared.

I quickly said, "I had to do a lot of freelancing work online, staying up late at night."

Her face showed that she believed me, but before she could ask more questions, I decided it was better to leave.

'I need to go,' I said, standing up from my chair. Sara tried to stop me, but I insisted, 'Don't worry about me. You finish your lunch. I have work to do.' Without waiting for her response, I walked out of the canteen.

How stupid was I? Sara was my best friend, and I'd been so lost in my own thoughts.

As I headed to my desk, I thought about calling Chirag. I dialed his number, but his phone was switched off.

Damn it! What now?

The ACP Shetty had said that the culprit would be caught soon, but I knew him. Chirag wouldn't go down easily. He'd destroy all the evidence. He killed Ramesh Reddy because he was going to inform the police about the robbery. In fact, Ramesh would name me for the robbery, but through me, the police would catch him.

My heart started pounding. I was the biggest proof of his crime. He could even kill me to keep me quiet. I was the only one who knew he went to Ramesh Reddy's house that night. I knew the hoodie and cap belonged to him. The police were already questioning me, and they could find him through me. I was the only thing standing between him and freedom.

How much did I even know about him? Hardly anything. We'd only been together a few days, and I let myself get close to him. That was my mistake. Why was his flat always locked from the outside? Whether I left for work in the morning or came home in the evening, it was always locked. Where did he go? I had no answers.

The only thing I knew was what he told me—that his parents died in an accident and he worked in Mumbai. But now, I couldn't believe a word he said. Just like the money and that night at Ramesh's house.

And how could I forget that apology video Ramesh Reddy made? I still remember his swollen face, beaten by Chirag. The ACP had said that before Ramesh Reddy was shot, he was badly beaten. But why? Why did Chirag help me with the money? Why take revenge on Ramesh? Maybe he had other intentions. Maybe he wanted to drag me into his criminal world, make me one of them.

I had to get rid of Chirag, no matter what. What could I do? It would have been better if I had gone to the police and told them everything about Chirag. But then, the police might have thought

I was his partner in crime. Oh, Chirag! I was trapped in his mess.

Desperate for a solution, I tried calling him again, but his phone was still switched off.

Meanwhile, I had a lot of office work to handle. I had to meet Mr Deshmukh and explain why the police had come to the office asking for me. On top of that, I faced another problem—a tough one. Some code broke down suddenly without any clear reason, and I spent the entire afternoon searching for a tiny mistake buried deep within hundreds of lines of code.

But while debugging the code, an idea struck me: a brilliant idea to deal with Chirag once and for all.

Yes, this could work.

Around 7:30 PM, Sara, some colleagues, and I left the office together to head home. Sara, concerned, told me, "Be brave! Don't let the police questioning bring you down. By the way, you look better now. There's a brightness in your eyes."

I smiled and said goodbye. Sara had no idea that I had a plan to bring Chirag, the liar and murderer, to justice. That's why my eyes sparkled.

I pretended to head toward my cab, but I had other plans. There was a big market near my office building. I hurried there, making sure no one noticed me. I was looking for something—an old-fashioned public phone booth. In this age when everyone uses mobile phones, it isn't easy to find one. But I had seen it before while coming and going to the office.

Finally, I spotted it. A small shop selling electrical items had a glass cabin in the corner, used as a telephone booth. It was exactly what I needed. My heart raced with the thrill of what I was about to do. Before entering the shop, I wrapped my face with a dupatta from my bag so the shopkeeper wouldn't recognize me.

"I need to make a phone call," I said to the shopkeeper. He nodded and pointed to the booth.

I stepped inside, took a deep breath, and picked up the landline phone, which was resting on a hangar. My heart was racing, but I dialed the police control room number, trying to calm myself down.

"Hello, I need to tell you about the robber who stole the cash from the lending company's office and the murderer of banker Ramesh Reddy," I said quickly.

I felt like Chirag was coming for me with the gun I had seen in a picture in his room. But the police operator didn't seem to care. He asked silly questions like who I was, where I was calling from, and how I knew all this. I interrupted him, "I don't have time! The killer could come after me at any moment. Just listen! He lives in a flat in a residential apartment in Brookfield. His flat number is..."

Suddenly, I heard a beep-beep-beep sound. Had the operator hung up on me? No, that couldn't be. Maybe the signal was lost, or the line was cut. Damn it!

I tried calling again, but there was no dial tone. Oh God! What was happening? I poked my head out of the cabin and asked the shop owner.

He sighed, "The line has been cutting out a lot lately. I complained, and the repairman came, but it would go dead again the next day. I'm fed up."

I was fed up too. What was wrong with me? Was God protecting Chirag? No, it felt like the devil was on his side. I couldn't tell the police the flat number or the name of the apartment. I had only said it was in Brookfield, but that area was huge with many apartments. What could the police do? I couldn't say.

Should I have called from somewhere else? No, I was done. I felt disappointed standing in the glass cabin. I had done all I could.

I stepped out of the glass cabin, and suddenly, I smelled a cigar behind me. I broke into a cold sweat. I felt the warmth of him near my ear as he whispered like a snake, "Ssss... you told the police about me. You don't trust your lover, dear."

I turned around, my face covered with a dupatta, leaving only my eyes exposed.

He continued, "You look good in that outfit. You can hide from the whole world, but not from me. I can find you just by your smell." Chirag sniffed like a dog.

He was different, not the Chirag I knew. He was smiling, his cigar sending out thick smoke. His brown eyes sparkled with cruelty, and his face looked more menacing than ever. Fear shot through me, and I didn't want to die—not by his hands. I turned and ran out of the shop.

Just then, I heard the shop owner shout, "What happened, ma'am? Give me my money for the phone call!" I turned back, and to my surprise, Chirag was gone.

Was I dreaming? What was happening to me, Rishika? This man was driving me crazy. Embarrassed, I handed the shop owner the money for the useless call, feeling defeated.

As I got closer to the Brookfield area near my apartment around 9 PM, I saw a lot of police cars and officers moving around. The police were using walkie-talkies to give orders, and the sirens were blaring.

I was wrong about the call I made. It turned out it wasn't useless at all.

At first, I didn't understand what was happening. Then, a thought hit me: it was all because of my call to the police control room. I wanted to find out what was going on, so I decided to ask some police officers. I stepped out of my cab after paying the fare and noticed two female constables standing by the road, chatting.

I hesitated for a moment, then asked, "What's going on here? Why are there so many police?"

"Ma'am, some terrorists are hiding in a flat in the area. We are here to catch them," one of them replied while the other looked at me intently.

Terrorists? My mind raced. I realized how quickly rumors could spread. The other constable then asked, "Do you live here?"

"Yes, I live in a flat nearby," I answered.

"Then take my advice seriously: stay somewhere else tonight. This area isn't safe for you. Anything could happen; these criminals can do anything," she spoke quietly as if she didn't want anyone else to hear.

I thought about the criminal. What could he do to me? I remembered how I had fallen for him. I loved him, kissed him, and slept with him, only to find out he was a robber and a murderer. Chirag, it would be better if the police caught you tonight and put you behind bars.

The thought filled my heart with sorrow. Would the police beat him? No, they wouldn't do that. Criminals have rights, too. What was I thinking?

But the constable was right; it wasn't safe for me to stay there. The police could be searching all night. What if I told them his flat number and the apartment name? It could end everything quickly. But no, what was I thinking? If I did that, everyone would know about me and what had happened with Chirag. I needed to stay away from him and from this police operation.

I turned back and headed to the cab.

• • •

I pressed the doorbell.

I stood outside Sara's flat, unsure of why I had come. I felt embarrassed for even thinking about it, but I had no choice. I had to stay the night.

Sara, the daughter of a famous criminal lawyer, Mr Vinod Rao, could have lived in her father's big bungalow in the city, but she preferred to rent her own flat because she wanted to be independent.

I pressed the doorbell again and heard footsteps coming closer. Sara opened the door, dressed in an orange sleeveless T-shirt and a dark blue skirt.

She welcomed me with a warm hug. I let out a deep sigh and hugged her back tightly, hoping she wouldn't do anything awkward like she had the last time I stayed over.

CHAPTER XI

Sara had ordered a large pizza, and her fridge was stocked with cold beer. That was our dinner—pizza and beer—while we watched the local news on her big 55-inch smart TV.

The news reporter was shouting into the mic, *"Look, the police search operation is happening right behind me. You can see how many officers are gathered, but so far, no suspicious person has been found. This search is led by ACP Arjun Shetty."*

As the camera caught a glimpse of ACP Arjun, he didn't seem interested in giving any news bites. He hurried with a few officers to a specific spot in the area.

The reporter, however, kept pushing for a statement. Finally, in a calm but irritated voice, ACP Arjun said, *"We received a call in the police control room. Someone reported that the criminal involved in a robbery and murder is hiding somewhere in Brookfield. That's why we've launched this operation."*

"But, sir, this is a large area, and there's no specific location for the criminal," the reporter insisted.

"The caller, a young woman, seemed to be in danger. She was trying to give more details, but the line got cut, or maybe the criminal silenced her. We can't say anything for sure yet. Let us do our job," ACP moved away with his team.

The TV news reporter looked straight into the camera and spoke in a serious tone.

"I have an interesting fact to share. A couple of months ago, a similar incident happened. Back then, a young woman called the

police control room with a tip about Saumitra Sen, the notorious criminal and serial killer from Bengal. He had been hiding here under a fake identity. Thanks to that local girl's information, the police were able to catch him."

"Is history repeating itself? Will the police capture the person behind this robbery and murder? To find out, stay tuned to our channel. Don't go anywhere!"

Sara and I sat there with our mouths open, staring at the screen. When the channel cut to a commercial break, Sara asked, "Who do you think that girl could be, the one who called the police?"

It was me. I swallowed hard. If the line hadn't cut, I would've told them exactly where the criminal, Chirag, was hiding.

"Maybe she was his partner in crime," Sara joked, noticing I wasn't answering.

"Maybe," I muttered, taking a big gulp of my beer.

Then, with a playful grin, Sara added, "But I have to say, ACP Arjun is quite something! He's so handsome and charming, especially in that uniform. He looked like a God of love!"

I couldn't believe how much her taste had changed. Now, she liked men. Well, at least it was a good thing for tonight since I was staying over.

After dinner, Sara and I went to bed. But this time, something was different. Unlike last time, she didn't ask me to stay with her or to hold her in my arms. Instead, she suggested I sleep in the other room. So, for the first time, we were in separate bedrooms.

I tried to push the idea away, but it kept coming back. I imagined Chirag running, the police right behind him.

Brookfield had become a trap for him. He would never escape. But I felt trapped, too, tangled in a web of my own.

What if Chirag surrendered? What if he confessed in court? After serving his time, he could become a good person, and I would be waiting for him when he got out. We'd get married, move far away, maybe near a lake, a forest, or a mountain, and have kids. We'd live happily ever after.

What a ridiculous idea! That would never happen.

ACP Arjun looked tough, and I knew he would catch Chirag eventually. What if they shot him in an encounter? I couldn't bear the thought of Chirag's body lying there, bloody and unclaimed on the road. The very idea made me sweat. No, this couldn't happen.

I needed to know what was going on. Maybe I could call my landlord and ask him for some information. I picked up my phone and dialed him, thankful that Sara was in the other room. She would have bombarded me with silly questions otherwise.

The landlord answered on the second ring, "Hello."

"Hello, uncle, what's happening over there?" I asked.

"Oh, the police have spoiled the night. They're searching every flat, every room. But they haven't found anything. It's a good thing you texted me about staying at your friend's place. I showed them your flat using the spare key. Don't worry, they didn't mess up your stuff."

I interrupted him, "Did the police check the flat next to mine?"

"Whose?"

"The one next to mine—Chirag's flat."

"Yes, yes. I told you they checked every flat, including his. I kept telling them—"

"What did they find?" I cut him off again, eager to know if they had found anything suspicious in Chirag's place.

"There? What could they have found? Just an old typewriter, some books, clothes, and nothing else. But why are you asking?"

I didn't want to answer him. "Okay, uncle. Thanks," I said and hung up.

I tried to sleep, but sleep was nowhere to be found. My body was tired, my mind even more so, after the long, exhausting day at the office. Yet, no matter how much I wanted to rest, my mind wouldn't stop replaying the day's events.

Scene by scene, it all drifted through my thoughts until, at last, sleep began to pull me in.

Then—Bang! Bang!

"Chirag!" I woke up shouting. I was sweating; my breath was heavy.

It was just a dream!

I reached for the water bottle on the table next to my bed and took a sip. I was relieved that Sara wasn't with me in the room; otherwise, I would have to explain why I was shouting Chirag's name.

What a horrible nightmare it was!

In the dream, there was a thunderstorm, and it was pouring rain. Chirag was running in the middle of the road, terrified. ACP Arjun was chasing him in a police van, like death itself hunting him down. Several other police vans surrounded Chirag, and without a word, ACP Arjun opened fire. Chirag fell to the ground, dead, with the rain drenching his lifeless body. The rain soaked him completely. It was such a horrible dream.

It was around 2:30 a.m., and I couldn't sleep anymore. I grabbed my phone and checked the news. But there was no update; the news still said the police search was ongoing.

I climbed out of bed and walked to the balcony. It was raining, and the thunderstorm was raging. The cool breeze felt calming. I remembered the night I first met Chirag. He had saved my life when I almost fell from the balcony of my ninth-floor apartment. The weather was just like this. I felt a deep pain in my chest, sorrow for Chirag. A heavy, aching pain.

I missed his kiss. He was good at kissing. I remember when he first kissed me. His lips gently touched mine, and my eyes closed. To remember that moment, I close my eyes and let my lips remember the taste of his lips—how beautiful it was!

What? What was I thinking? What an absurd thing! Now, I have come to know that he was a criminal—a murderer.

Suddenly, a raindrop fell on my lips, and I opened my eyes. My heart skipped a beat when I saw Chirag.

He was standing on the road below. He was under the shop's shed to avoid the rain. There was a little bulb over his head. He was smiling and smoking his favorite cigar. I was terrified to see him there in front of me. The thick smoke of the cigar made him more mysterious.

My heart started beating fast, and I thought of running away from there. I didn't want to see him at all. I ran from the balcony toward the room. Shivering with fear, I sat down on the edge of the bed.

Could he come to this room? No. The main door of the flat was closed. The door of this room was closed, too. He couldn't come here.

Ten minutes passed. I thought he would have gone away by now. Then I heard a thud on the balcony as if someone had jumped onto it. I saw his shadow on the other side of the balcony glass. Keeping my heartbeats under control, I tried to close the sliding glass door of the balcony.

But he held it with his strong hand from the other side. I tried my best but failed. The door was open now. He was in the room. I ran out of the room, screaming. But my scream got trapped in my throat as he slapped his strong hand over my mouth, pressing me back hard against the wall.

There was complete darkness in the room, only the light was coming from the streetlamp in the distance. Suddenly, a thunderstorm broke out. In the flash of lightning, his face appeared before me.

He looked terrifying. Now, he was going to kill me. My face turned pale, and I collapsed.

• • •

"Rishika, it's me, Chirag," he shook my shoulders quickly, trying to wake me up.

Slowly, I opened my eyes, still trying to figure out what had happened. Seeing him there, so close, I felt a jolt of shock and confusion. How long had I been like this? I noticed I was lying on a bed—Chirag must have brought me here. He sat beside me, his face full of worry. My emotions swirled. Fear gripped me, yet I felt an urge to hold him tight.

Tears filled my eyes as I stared at him, my voice trembling. "Why do you want to kill me?"

He looked at me with a confused smile. "What are you saying, sweetie? I don't want to kill you."

I shook my head, not believing him. "I don't believe you."

He sighed, his voice soft and reassuring. "Believe me, how could I ever harm you? You're my life. How could I ever hurt my own life?" His words were like a warm breeze, and I felt myself wavering.

"But if you don't want to hurt me, then why did you slap your hand over my mouth?" I asked, my voice shaking.

He glanced at me, a calm expression on his face. "I did it to keep you quiet... so your friend Sara wouldn't wake up. If she did, she'd ask too many questions and make things harder."

"How did you get here, right onto the balcony?" I asked.

"From the rain pipe," he said.

What? Why would he risk climbing up to the fifth floor using the rain pipe? What if he fell? I wanted to ask all these questions, but I stayed silent. I had to be strong. The man sitting beside me was a criminal. Even though I had feelings for him, I forced myself to keep control of my emotions.

"Why did you come here? Go away. Get lost. I don't want to see your face!"

"Why are you saying this? We love each other," his voice was filled with emotion.

"I don't love you anymore."

"Why?"

"Because you're a murderer. And not just that, you're a robber, too." I spat on his face.

"Who told you that?" His voice was calm like nothing had happened.

"The police. They showed a photo of the killer from the CCTV footage, and it was you. You tried to hide your face with a hoodie, but I recognized you. It was the same hoodie you wore when you went to Ramesh Reddy's house that night. And the police said the same person in the footage was involved in a robbery case, too." I rushed to say everything in one breath.

"Did the police show any photo or video where I was actually shooting Reddy?"
I did not reply.

"I admit that the person in the CCTV footage was me, but I didn't kill Ramesh. I was caught on camera because I went to his house that night, but I didn't kill him," he said. His brown eyes were serious, telling me he was telling the truth.

He continued, "I went to talk to him about the money I gave you. Yes, I beat him up because he was insulting you. I even made an apology video for you. Then I left. Ramesh was shot after I left."

"Then what about the robbery case?"

"I didn't do it. I told you that before."

"Then why did the police say that the person in the hoodie at both crime scenes was the same?"

"It was a trick by the police."

"ACP said Ramesh Reddy called the police, claiming he had information about the robber, and in return, the robber killed him."

"That might be true. Actually, it was true. The real robber somehow knew Ramesh Reddy was about to expose his identity, so he shot him dead."

"But Ramesh Reddy didn't know anything about the robber. He just suspected me of the robbery," I said.
"Yeah, you're right. Ramesh Reddy didn't have any information about the robber. He only wanted to frame you. But the real robber thought Ramesh Reddy knew too much, so he killed him," he said with a sigh, "Poor Ramesh Reddy."

"Are you telling the truth?"

"Yes, I am. Believe me."

"Then why did you run away when the police released the CCTV footage on the news?"

"I didn't run anywhere. I only saw the footage this afternoon in a grocery shop," he replied.

"Do you know what happened to me? The police came to my office. They asked why Ramesh had called me so late at night. I was the last person he spoke to before he was shot. After that, I saw the CCTV footage in my office. I recognized you. Do you know what happened to me then? I needed to talk to you. I needed the truth from you right then. But your phone was off. Why was your phone off all day?" I cried as I spoke.

He reached out to hug me, but I stepped back, not wanting to be close to him.

"Rishika," hearing my name from him felt like a sweet melody to my ears. He went on, "My phone was out of order this morning when I was at the gym. I gave it for repair, and I'll get it back tomorrow. I'm sorry. I understand what you must've been going through, but I..." He opened his arms for a hug again. This time, I couldn't say no.

It felt amazing to be in his arms. I could feel his heart beating against me. How foolish I was! I had been wrong all along. Chirag was no longer the criminal I thought he was.

"So, that's why your phone was off. I thought you had run away from the police," I said.

"Yes," he replied softly, brushing his fingers through my hair.

I asked again, "But how did you find me? What made you come here?"

"You didn't come home at the usual time from work, so I started worrying about you. Without my phone, I couldn't call. I thought maybe you were still at the office, but when I went there, it was closed. The guards said everyone had left at the usual time. I started to panic, not knowing where you were. I went to all the grocery stores, even to Cyrus' Corner, but you weren't there. My worry just grew, and eventually, I went back to my flat. Late at night, I had an idea – maybe you were staying with your friend Sara. So, I came here. You don't know, but I stood at that spot for over an hour, waiting for you."

Hearing this, my heart melted. He had searched the whole city for me, and here I was, thinking the worst about him.

How could I have been so wrong? I silently prayed, "God, forgive my mistakes."

"If you were standing there, under the shed of the shop, why didn't you come to the flat?" I asked, my voice tinged with confusion.

He looked at me with wide, innocent eyes and replied, "I thought you and Sara were both asleep after such a tiring day at the office. I didn't want to disturb your sleep."

His words were so sweet, so genuine that a warm smile spread across my face. Without thinking, I pulled him into a tight hug, realizing how wrong I had been to doubt him. It was then that I knew I had to tell him what I had done.

CHAPTER XII

Chirag was stunned by everything I said. His face tightened with anger as he spoke, "Rishika, do you even realize what you've done? Do you know how much trouble you could've caused me? It would've been better if the call had just cut off right then instead of you telling everything about me without even caring that I might not be guilty."

"I thought you were guilty," I replied, my voice trembling. "I couldn't get any answers from you, so I decided to go to the police."

"I was stupid. I know," I added, tears spilling down my cheeks. "I'm sorry. I'll never do this again. Please don't stay angry with me." I couldn't say anything else; the words caught in my throat.

He looked at me with a soft gaze. "I'm not angry with you," he said quietly, wiping my tears away. Then he leaned closer, his beard brushing against my neck, sending a shiver down my spine. His warmth seeped into my skin, and I let go of everything, sinking into his strong arms.

We kissed, the world around us fading as the moment consumed us.

The rain was pouring down heavily, like cats and dogs. He smiled playfully and said, "Why don't we go out on the balcony to enjoy the rain?" I liked the idea, so I agreed. He lifted me in his arms and carried me to the balcony. We sat there on the floor, arms around each other, watching the rain while the whole city was asleep.

"I'm hungry," he suddenly said. "I know it's late, but I can't help it."

"Baby's hungry!" I laughed and got up. "I'll get you something."

I hurried to the kitchen, passing by Sara's room. The door was locked from the inside, and I could hear her loud snores. I smiled, knowing she was fast asleep, then went to the kitchen. I didn't want to cook anything and risk waking her up, so I opened the fridge and found some ice cream. Perfect.

I returned with the ice cream and said, "Sorry, baby, this is all I could find." He grinned when he saw the tub of butterscotch. "I love this idea—ice cream and rain!"

We sat together, but I realized I'd forgotten to bring a spoon. He didn't care. Instead, he started eating the ice cream with his fingers, enjoying it like a little kid. I couldn't help but smile as I watched him. He offered me some, his fingers covered in ice cream. I didn't want the ice cream; I wanted to taste his fingers instead.

It felt incredible. A familiar warmth spread through me. I offered him some ice cream in the same way, and he slowly licked my fingers. The ice cream was gone, but he didn't stop licking. I didn't want him to ever stop.

The storm outside was loud, and the air felt electric. We sat there, staring at each other, the tension growing. He smiled and, without warning, spread some ice cream on my neck. The cold made me shiver, but his warm lips followed, and I gasped, feeling a spark inside me.

We didn't say anything. Without thinking, we moved closer, our playful moment turning into something more intense. Right there on the balcony, we started taking off each other's clothes, almost like we were in a race. The storm raged around us, but we were lost in our own world, the heat between us building with every second.

It was wild, it was intense, and in that moment, it felt like nothing else mattered.

• • •

14th October, Wednesday.

"Rishika!" Sara was yelling in my dream. But why?

"Rishika!" she shouted again, louder this time.

No, wait— it wasn't a dream. She was really yelling. I slowly opened my eyes, feeling dazed.

"Rishika, wake up." Why was she waking me up like this? I felt her leg against my side—no, not touching—kicking me. Why was she kicking me awake in my own home?

I forced my eyes fully open, realizing with a jolt—this wasn't my place. It was Sara's. Sunlight streamed in through the balcony. I glanced over, horrified to see my clothes scattered all over the balcony floor. I was wrapped in nothing but a blanket, completely unclothed underneath.

What had happened? I remembered last night. Chirag had come over. We'd cleared up our misunderstandings and ended up on the balcony together, losing ourselves to the moment. But now he was gone, leaving me in this mess.

"Rishika, what's wrong with you? Are you insane? Look at this disaster!" Sara's tone was sharp, using my full name—which only happened when she was furious. Otherwise, she'd just call me "Rishi."

"I'm… sorry," I muttered, my cheeks burning, as I tried to gather my scattered undergarments while still wrapped in the blanket.

"Sorry, my foot," she snapped.

I looked up, meeting her red, angry eyes. She leaned in, her voice rising, "If you wanted to have ice cream, eat it like a normal person! What kind of fantasy were you living out here on my balcony, half-naked? You can do whatever you want with your ice cream 'games' inside but out here…" She lowered her voice to a whisper. "You know, my maid woke me up, saying my 'friend'—meaning you—was lying on the balcony floor half-dressed!"

I glanced at the floor, feeling my face burn with shame. An empty ice cream box lay there, its contents smeared across the tiles. Memories of last night's ice cream "adventure" with Chirag flooded back, and for a second, I nearly laughed.

But Sara cut me off. "Why are you smiling?" she demanded. "Get inside, now! Change in the room before anyone else sees and starts gossiping to my father!"

Annoyed but too embarrassed to argue, I picked up my clothes and shuffled back to the room, still wrapped in the blanket. While I dressed, Sara gave her maid instructions on how to clean the balcony. The maid shot me a withering look as she passed, adding another layer of shame to the morning.

Once I was dressed, I thought it was over, but Sara wasn't done with me.

"Now tell me, what was going on?" she demanded.

I took a breath. There was no point in hiding it. "Chirag came over last night, and we…"

"Oh, God, not again, Rishi," she groaned, holding her head, watching me with a mix of frustration and concern.

"What? What's wrong?"

"Rishi, snap out of this Chirag fantasy and face reality. It's time for work," she stormed toward the door, then turned back and said, "Hurry up; breakfast is ready, and I've called a cab. We need to get to the office."

Half an hour later, we were sitting in a cab on our way to the office. We hadn't spoken since Sara told me breakfast was ready and called for the cab. We faced opposite directions—I was looking out the window, and she was glued to her phone. Or maybe she was just pretending to be busy.

Something wasn't right. Her behavior in her apartment didn't sit well with me. I wanted to ask her what was going on, but I kept quiet, not wanting to cause a scene in the cab. I replayed her words in my mind: "Get out of your Chirag fantasy and face reality." What did she mean by that? Why was she so angry this morning? She'd yelled at me like I was her servant. I felt like I knew what was bothering her.

Maybe she'd seen me and Chirag together late last night on her balcony. She must have watched us in a private moment, and now her jealousy was spilling out. Her morning anger had been her frustration unleashed. She knew I loved Chirag, and it was tearing her up inside.

The cab pulled up, and we both stepped out. I couldn't wait any longer – I had to get to the bottom of this.

"What's your problem?" I snapped at Sara as she rushed to catch the office lift.

She turned around, her chubby face looked puffy, and she said, "I don't have a problem, sweetie. *You're* the one with the problem." She pointed her finger at me.

"Oh really? Care to explain, madam?" I stood with my arms crossed, not at all in a hurry to punch in for work.

She took a deep breath, watching as the lift doors closed and it started moving up without her. Her face turned red. "The problem is Chirag!"

Of course, I knew Sara hated Chirag because he'd saved me from her controlling grip and labeled me as 'homo' to push me away.

While I was lost in my thoughts, Sara darted to another lift that had just arrived on the ground floor. I ran after her—not to rush to the office, but to get answers from her.

The lift was packed. I stood by the doors, and Sara was squeezed at the back. Our eyes met briefly before we looked away.

The lift stopped on the fifth floor. I punched in my card, and then Sara punched in hers. I went to my desk to drop my handbag and hurried back to Sara, who was just settling at her desk.

"Chirag isn't my..." I started, but Sara quickly cut me off, waving her hand to silence me. She pointed toward the empty conference room. I realized it was probably better that she wanted this conversation privately—not in front of everyone. If they overheard, the whole office would know she was gay.

I stepped into the conference room, and Sara followed, shutting the door with a sharp slam.

"What were you saying?" she asked, her eyes drilling into mine.

"I was saying that Chirag isn't my problem. He's... he's my love," I replied, holding her gaze.

She laughed, a sharp, mocking sound. "Oh, so now Chirag is your lover?" She moved closer, her face turning serious as she continued, "Come on, Rishi. Face reality. Chirag isn't for you." She reached out, her hand brushing my hair and face. I could see something deeper in her eyes.

I pulled my face away. "What reality? Should I just turn gay like you?"

Her face went red as if I'd hit a nerve. She shouted, "What are you saying, girl?"

"Yes, I'm saying it right. You're gay, and you wanted me to join your circle," I accused, my voice rising. "That's why you didn't want me to be with a guy—like Chirag."

She looked at me, clearly irritated. "How did you even come to this conclusion that I'm gay?"

"Remember that night I stayed at your flat, sharing the same bed? In the middle of the night, you started kissing me... touching me..." I trailed off, feeling anger mixed with hurt.

"Stop this nonsense, Rishika!" she cut me off, practically spitting the words. "What garbage is in your mind? It wasn't me. You were the one who kissed me that night, looking for... more."

"What? I can't believe this, Sara. How can you lie like this? You're just trying to blame me for your own actions."

"I'm not lying, Rishika! Wake up and face the truth! This is why, last night, when you came over, I offered you another room to sleep in—not with me."

So, my best friend Sara turned out to be a liar. I thought she was my biggest support, but she ended up betraying me in the worst way possible. To hide her own identity, she accused me of being gay.

Sara looked annoyed, muttering something under her breath.

"Stop mumbling and say it clearly," I demanded, feeling a painful weight in my chest.

"...that's why my father told me not to stay with you," she finally said, a hint of frustration in her voice. "I told him your 'truth', but I was still trying to look out for you... and now you're blaming me for something so ridiculous."

I shouted back, "If your rich father didn't want you around me, why did you keep following me everywhere?" I fought back my tears and told her firmly, "Stay away from me."

"Yes, I should definitely stay away from you," Sara said, her voice sharp. "After seeing you lying naked on my balcony this morning, I knew it. And what were you doing with the ice cream last night? I still don't get it. You had ice cream smeared all over you! Were you trying out some kind of... Kama Sutra fantasy with ice cream?"

Sara's words felt like nails stabbing into my ears. I couldn't believe how much I had to listen to her just to stay in her flat. It was all my fault. God must be punishing me for what I did to Chirag.

I had completely misunderstood Chirag, thinking he was a criminal. I even called the police on him. Luckily, the call got disconnected before I could say anything. I didn't want to imagine what would have happened to him if it hadn't. But now, I felt this was my punishment—payback for the harm I almost caused Chirag.

Lost in these heavy thoughts, I didn't notice Sara standing near me. I didn't even want to look at her. She said softly, from a few steps away, "Rishi, I'm not your enemy. I care about you. You should see Dr. Neelam."

"Shut up, you bitch!" I spat out, fury rising in me. "Get lost! And take your Dr. Neelam with you. Is she part of your circle, too? Is that why you keep pushing her on me?"

Sara didn't have the courage to look at me after that. She left without saying another word.

CHAPTER XIII

How long had I been sleeping? My whole body felt stiff and sore. Why couldn't I move my hands? It was like they were trapped behind me. My legs were straight, locked in place too. Was it day or night? I had no way of knowing.

How long had it been since I'd had water? My lips were parched, my tongue dry as sandpaper. I tried to lick my lips, but my tongue wouldn't move. There was something in my mouth – a cloth tied tight.

Slowly, I forced my eyes open. Darkness. Had I gone blind? No, I realized—a woolen cap was pulled down over my face, blocking my sight. My mouth gagged, my hands tied behind me, my legs bound. I could hardly breathe.

Oh, God. It hit me like a punch to the gut. I had been kidnapped!

The place that once felt lively and safe suddenly changed the moment I realized I was a prisoner there. My heart pounded with the need to escape, to break free. The thought of being someone's captive ate away at my sense of self, making me question everything. I couldn't help but wonder, *how long had I been here?*

I needed to remember, to put the pieces together, to hold on to every detail of what had happened to me. But how had I even ended up here?

Trying to think straight wasn't easy, not with the sharp pain throbbing in the back of my head. The ache was terrible, unlike anything I'd ever felt. I braced myself, trying to push my body with all the strength I had, but nothing happened. All I felt was the wound on my head burning, pulsing with horrible pain.

I needed to remember what had happened.

I had to focus on what happened just hours ago.

I remembered a beautiful night with Chirag. We were on our tiny balcony, playing with our ice cream while rain poured down like cats and dogs. It was late, and we were both laughing, enjoying the moment.

The next morning, Sara showed up, yelling at me under the bright sun as we headed to the office together. Later, in the conference room, things heated up between us, and we ended up in a full-blown argument. I was furious after that.

Back at my desk, I was so frustrated that I started throwing things around, taking my anger out on my colleagues over silly issues. I couldn't stop thinking that they might complain about me to HR, Kamini Duggal.

I had to deal with that old, plump woman who always looked at me with her glasses balanced on the tip of her nose, ready to slip. Kamini's mouth fell open in shock when she saw the anger on my face in her office. It was beyond my control. How could anyone stay calm after her best friend betrayed her and blamed her for something she didn't do?

By evening, an email arrived: I'd been given a one-month notice from the company. Sara must have been thrilled, seeing me tossed out. It didn't matter how much code I'd written for our projects or how many sleepless nights I'd spent creating powerful presentations to impress our clients. Nothing mattered now.

It was fine. I didn't need to be around people who were so fake. No one there was truly a friend. After leaving, I took a cab back to my apartment complex. As I was crossing the road to my building, I heard someone call my name from behind. I turned around—and in that instant, something struck the back of my head.

After that, everything went black.

I had been kidnapped.

Who was behind my kidnapping? Could it be you, Sara? You wanted me to join your group, and when I refused, you took matters into your own hands. And Dr. Neelam... was she involved too? Was this gang of girls trying to make me one of them? No, Sara, you could see that I wasn't like you. I begged her to let me go. I wanted to get to Chirag. I'd leave this city and start fresh somewhere else with him. I wanted to be with him forever.

I felt footsteps approaching. Voices drifted closer. The terror was real. I couldn't see, couldn't speak, couldn't move. My body lay limp on the floor like a discarded sack. I jerked when I heard a man's voice in the distance.

"Boss, she's starting to come to."

I swore at that moment — if my mouth was freed, if my face cover was removed, I would scream Sara's name loud enough for the whole world to hear. Sara, I would expose you!

The cloth covering my face was yanked off. Blinking under the flickering tube light above me, I saw two men through the strands of my messy hair. One of them, sitting casually on a cheap plastic chair, looked about thirty-five or so. He had fair skin, a gym-toned body, and sharp, handsome features. He wore an expensive suit with a tie, his hair neatly gelled back, and his face was clean-shaven. I didn't recognize him.

But the other man was different. His skin was dark, his pale eyes piercing, and his face was rough and weathered. I'd seen him before somewhere—yet I couldn't remember where.

The boss's eyes gleamed with desire as he said, "She's so damn sexy! Are you sure this is the girl we've been searching for?"

"Yes, boss. I met her and questioned her in her office."

Then it hit me – I recognized the other man. He was SI Vijay. He had come to my office a few days ago to question me about Reddy's murder. I didn't recognize him at first because, back then, he wore his police uniform. Here, he looked like any ordinary man, dressed in plain clothes.

But why was a policeman like Vijay here? It looked like he was part of this kidnapping too. That meant Vijay was working with this 'boss,' but I still didn't know who this man really was.

The boss turned to Vijay and said, "Make her sit."

I was held by my back like a sack being dragged across the floor. My feet were bound tightly with rope, making it hard to stand. I stumbled and was pulled toward the chair. I was made to sit in front of the boss. Vijay reached forward and gently touched my hair, trying to move it out of my face.

My mouth was gagged with cloth and rope, so I turned my face away, resisting his touch. Vijay smiled, a chilling grin. He bent down and picked up the hairband that had fallen on the floor. Then, without warning, he came behind me. His hand gripped my hair tightly, and with a cruel force, he pulled my hair back and secured it with the band, his grip strong and unforgiving.

I had no choice but to endure all of this. I looked around at my surroundings. It felt like I was in an old chemical factory that should have been closed a long time ago. Everywhere I looked, I saw huge containers, dusty bottles of chemicals, and wires hanging loosely. The place was dimly lit by old bulbs and flickering tube lights, so I could tell it was night.

I locked eyes with the two of them, feeling pain from the wound on my head. My legs and hands were tightly bound, and my mouth was gagged.

"Give her water," the Boss said, smiling.

Vijay stepped forward with a bottle of water. I needed it badly. My lips were dry and cracked, black from dehydration. He untied the cloth from my mouth and placed the water near my lips. I drank like an animal, bound and helpless. Tears welled up in my eyes as I saw how far I had fallen.

After drinking, I felt a small surge of energy, but my voice was weak as I whispered, "Who are you? Why am I here like this?"

Vijay's voice was cold as he said, "He is Mr Raj Reddy—the owner of CredZone. Remember CredZone?"

I did. CredZone was the lending company whose office had been robbed of a huge amount of cash.

"Now, tell us, baby, where is the rest of the money?" he demanded.

I was too weak to respond, barely able to speak, "What are you talking about?"

"Don't test my patience," Boss shouted, his face turning red with rage. He was no longer smiling.

"Please, let me go. I swear, I don't know anything about the money," I pleaded, my voice trembling.

Vijay leaned in close, his breath hot on my face. "You don't know about the money, huh? You liar. The cash you returned to Mr Ramesh Reddy came from CredZone. The company uses a white paper strip to bundle all cash. The company's name is printed on it in very tiny letters that are impossible to read with the eye. The white paper strip matches exactly—the same cash that was stolen and the same cash you handed to Ramesh Sir."

The pain in my head was unbearable, and as I tried to process what I was hearing, it felt like my mind was screaming in agony.

"And when my elder brother, Mr. Ramesh Reddy, threatened you and told you to go to the police, you killed him!" Raj shouted. His voice echoed through the factory, sending a chill down my spine. Raj was Ramesh Reddy's younger brother.

"I didn't kill anyone," I managed to say, my voice barely a whisper, drained of all energy.

"If you had met me before all of this, I would have never believed what people said about you," the Boss spoke softly, his voice almost soothing. "I would have made you the queen of my heart." He paused, then continued with a wicked grin, "But it's not too late. Just give me the rest of the money, and I'll set you free. You'll be mine forever." His words dripped with lust.

"What about the rest of the money?" Vijay yelled. "The robbery was for forty-five lakh rupees, not just twenty! Raj Sir told the police it was a smaller amount to protect himself from the tax authorities. But the truth is, it was forty-five lakh. You gave Ramesh Sir twenty-five lakh, so where's the rest of the money, sweetie?"

"I had no idea about the money," I said, my voice shaking. "It was given to me by one of my friends."

"Oh, your friend must be a millionaire to just hand over twenty-five lakh like it's nothing," Vijay sneered. "You think I'm stupid? Don't try to fool me."

"I'm telling the truth! Please believe me," I pleaded.

Without warning, Vijay slapped me across the face. He was seething with anger, "Do you expect me to believe you? You are a lying bitch!"

His slap was so forceful that it split the edge of my lip, and I could feel warm blood trickling down.

The boss stepped in, his voice calm but cold. "Vijay, hold on," he said. Then he turned his gaze to me, his eyes burning. "If I believe you and this friend gave you all the money, then tell me his name because it sounds like he's the real thief and the one who killed my brother. Just give me the name of that bastard."

Now, it seemed so easy. All I had to do was say the name, and they would let me go. Just a simple exchange. But for me, it wasn't simple at all. I couldn't bring myself to say the name—Chirag. I couldn't make the same mistake I nearly made before. I wasn't about to tell them that Chirag had given me the money. I couldn't risk them going after him. He was the one I loved, and I had to protect him. This was my only chance to fix what I'd done wrong.

So, I lied. "It was J.K.," I said, giving them the name they wanted to hear—my colleague, J.K., from work.

"You're lying, you little—!" Vijay yelled, raising his boot as if he was about to kick me. But just then, Raj stopped him, "Hold on, Vijay," he ordered.

Vijay glared at me, his voice dripping with anger. "Sir, she's making things up. Who would give her twenty-five lakh rupees?"

"I didn't know where I found the courage, but I spoke up loudly. 'J.K. is launching a new tech start-up, and he wants me on board badly. I told him I'd only work with him if he gave me that amount as an advance. In exchange, I agreed to work for him without pay for five years. He accepted, and we signed a contract."

I was making it all up as I went along, saying whatever came to mind.

My words had convinced them. They looked at each other, exchanging a glance that told me they believed me.

"Where can we find J.K.?" Vijay asked, his tone sharp. "We'll grab that son of a bitch."

Ah, this was a whole new problem. Now, I had to protect my colleague, J.K. I didn't even like him; his crude jokes during meetings made me cringe. But if I didn't act quickly, they'd hunt him down. They'd sit him right next to me, and then my entire secret would be out. That would be dangerous—for Chirag especially.

"He's not in town right now," I said, lying smoothly. "He's in Delhi, trying to get some license approved by the authorities."

"When is he coming?"

"He'll be here by tomorrow evening," I said, trying to keep my voice steady even as my chest tightened.

They exchanged a glance, as if they were communicating without words. Then, out of nowhere, Raj stood up, and Vijay followed. I had no idea what was happening. Were they leaving?

"Now what? Let me go! I've told you everything I know."

Vijay paused and turned back to me. "Oh, don't worry, sweetheart. You'll be right here when your J.K. shows up," he flashed a cruel grin, his yellow teeth glinting, "and in total darkness."

I screamed as they left, but they just kept walking. Those bastards shut off all the lights in the abandoned factory. I was left alone, tied tightly to a chair, my wrists and ankles bound. But at least my mouth was free – I could still yell.

But for how long? How long would my dry throat hold out? And who would even hear me in this forgotten place?

I had screamed for help with every bit of strength I had left. But there was no answer. It felt like I was the only person left on Earth, talking to myself, with no one to hear me.

Parched and helpless, I sank into unconsciousness.

CHAPTER XIV

Was I dead? No. I could still breathe. My eyes were closed, but I could feel it—I was alive. Weakly, I called out, "Please...someone...let me go. Can anyone hear me?"

"Yes, Rishika, I'm here for you," Chirag whispered softly, so close to my ear.

I thought I was dreaming. Maybe Chirag had somehow found me in the place where the kidnappers had kept me. I felt his gentle hand brush my hair. I opened my eyes, and to my surprise, it wasn't a dream. Chirag was really there, sitting near me.

But wait... where was I? I looked around. I was in my room. Shocked, I jumped up from the bed. I was lying in my own bed. This had to be a dream, right? How could I be here? In a panic, I slapped myself to see if I was dreaming. Ouch! That hurt. It was real.

Chirag laughed and said, "It's real, Rishika. You're free from those bastards."

I couldn't believe what he said. "But how?"

"I saved you—my life," his brown eyes sparkled with joy and pride.

"Hey, Chirag!" I hugged him tightly, but as I did, I winced in pain. "Aah." My hands, tightly bound for so long, were swollen and hurt badly.

Chirag pulled me away and examined my hands carefully. Then, he grabbed a tube of ointment from the first aid box on the floor. He looked so caring as he gently applied the ointment to my wounds. I was surprised that he had the first aid kit ready for me.

He worked quickly, applying ointment to my legs where the rope had been and then to the cut at the corner of my mouth, a wound from Vijay's slap. The sting made me flinch, and I felt tears well up as I remembered the humiliation I'd suffered in that abandoned factory.

"I swear, Rishika, I'll tear the skin off the man who did this to you," Chirag's brown eyes burned with fury.

"I don't need all this," I said softly, "just stay close to me." I kissed his hand as he gently applied ointment to my bruises. I wanted him to know everything that had happened, so I began.

"I was just crossing the road to come home. It was later than usual," I hesitated, not wanting to tell him about the hard day at work or how I'd stopped by a nearby bar to unwind before heading home.

I took a shaky breath and continued, "When I got close to the apartment, I heard someone call my name. I turned, and then—" I swallowed, feeling the memory rush back. "Someone hit me hard on the back of my head. The next thing I knew, I woke up in that abandoned factory. My hands and legs were tied, and my mouth was stuffed with thick cloth."

I shivered, the fear returning as I spoke.

"And I already know all of this."

Surprised, I asked, "What? How could you know?"

He looked at me, his voice filled with worry. "I was on the balcony of my flat when it happened. I saw two men throw you into a black van.

I was terrified—I couldn't believe what I was seeing."

I ran my fingers gently through his hair, urging him to go on. He took a breath and said, "I rushed down to the ground floor, but by then, the van had vanished. Luckily, an auto driver nearby had seen it, too, disappearing down the road. I hopped into his auto, and we followed, hoping to catch up."

He paused, pain flickering in his eyes. "But we lost it. Hours passed before I finally found that van, parked on a deserted road outside an old, abandoned factory."

He looked at me and said, "I was just about to go inside when I saw a BMW coming out of the factory. I quickly searched the car's number online to find out who owned it. That's when I realized it belonged to Ramesh Reddy. But he was dead, so it had to be someone from his family driving it..."

"It was Raj Reddy, Ramesh's younger brother, along with Sub-Inspector Vijay," I told him.

Chirag sighed softly. "I'm sorry, Rishika. I was too late. You had to put up with all their torture and nonsense."

"Why are you saying sorry, baby?" I asked, curiosity sparking in my voice. "You set me free—that's all that matters. But how did you manage it? I thought I was in Raj's custody, guarded by his goons."

"Yes, you were," Chirag replied with a proud smile. "But Raj's men relaxed once his BMW drove away. I slipped in through a back exit I found near the factory wall. I climbed over and got inside. You were there in the hall, tied up and unconscious. I picked you up and carried you out, careful not to alert his men."

"Hey!" I said, trying to sound cheerful. "How lucky I am to have you, Chirag."

He smiled and replied, "I think I'm even luckier."

"But you brought me here... I don't think it's safe. Raj and his goons could come looking for me," I said, my voice trembling.

"Don't worry, Rishika," he reassured me. "If they come, they'll face me."

"Chirag, you're amazing," I muttered, shaking my head in disbelief.

"Now, tell me, Rishika. What do they want from you? Why did Raj and his men kidnap you?" he asked, his expression turning serious, with a hint of anger in his eyes.

I began explaining everything that had happened between Raj, Vijay, and me.

"Rishika, why didn't you just tell them I gave you all that money? You shouldn't have named your colleague, J.K."

"I was trying to protect you, sweetheart."

"But now things are even more complicated," he sounded anxious.

"I was scared for you back then. Raj looked dangerous, and Vijay—he seemed even worse."

"They're both partners in crime," Chirag said, his tone serious. "I found out from my sources. CredZone that lending company was actually run on dirty money. Raj and his older brother, Ramesh Reddy, were behind it. They took black money from the wealthy and turned it clean by pretending to give loans to the poor. All the money stolen from CredZone was black. That's why Raj didn't report the actual amount to the police."

I looked into his eyes and said, "Raj was saying that the money I gave to Ramesh—the money you gave me—has the same special white strip as the cash stolen from CredZone."

He hesitated, rubbing his chin. "W-what did he say?" he stammered. "This has to be a setup. I think Raj and Vijay are trying to pin both the robbery and the murder on you. That's why Raj was so curious if anyone was helping you. He wants to drag anyone involved into this mess."

"Those men are ruthless," I murmured, feeling a chill run through me.

He met my eyes, his voice steady. "Rishika, I'm convinced now—Raj is behind his own brother Ramesh's murder."

My breath caught. "How can you be so sure, Chirag?"

Chirag looked at me and said, "Rishika, when I went to Dinesh's house on Monday night, he was on the phone with someone. They were arguing—really intense. I remember Ramesh shouting, *'You're not my brother anymore. You're my biggest enemy. You betrayed me.'* At the time, I didn't think much of it, but now it's clear: things weren't right between the Reddy brothers."

I listened with my mouth wide open. "You're right, Chirag. We should tell all of this to the police and finally get free from these criminals."

"Don't be childish, Rishika," Chirag said, a bit angry. "The police have footage of me wearing a hoodie near Ramesh's house. They think I'm the one who killed him. And Ramesh's brother, Raj, has enough money to make sure I end up behind bars. Rishika, remember, if you have money, you can bend the rules."

He paused, then added, "And to top it off, SI Vijay is on Raj's side. He'll use every trick in the book to keep me locked up for good. I could handle prison, Rishika, but they'd frame you too. That's something I won't allow."

Chirag was right. I had to let go of the idea of going to the police.

"Then, Chirag," I asked, "how are we going to deal with these criminals—Raj and Vijay?"

I could see a fierce determination in Chirag's eyes as he spoke. "Rishika, Raj wants to know who gave you the money. So, I'm going to tell them."

"No!" I cried out without thinking.

"Rishika, stop it. Don't shout," he said, firm and serious.

"You can't go to them."

"I have to. They treated you so badly in that factory, and I need to make them pay."

Raj got up from the bed, his face clouded with fear. Desperately, I pleaded, "No, Chirag, don't go. They have dangerous men."

"Come on, Rishika. This won't end if I don't face them."

"Please, Chirag... don't go. Let's leave instead. We'll move to a new city, start fresh, and be happy together."

"Rishika, we'll go wherever you want. But right now, I have to leave for them," Chirag said.

"No, Chirag! If you step out of this flat tonight, I'll jump off this balcony. I mean it!" I replied, breathing heavily. I couldn't let him leave. I didn't want him to go to them. I couldn't lose him.

Chirag came closer, kissed me gently, and whispered, "What are you saying, baby? Don't say that again. I'm not going anywhere." He pulled me into a hug.

I whispered, "But you are going... to the kitchen."

He looked confused. "For what?"

"I'm starving. Really, really starving."

With a chuckle, he said, "Alright, madam, I'll head to the kitchen and whip up something quick for your hunger."

I lay on the bed, lost in my thoughts. Memories flooded back—what happened at the factory when Raj and his goons kidnapped me, the chaos at the office, and the fallout with Sara. I hadn't even told Chirag yet that I'd been given a one-month notice at work. Soon, I'd be jobless.

Fifteen minutes later, Chirag returned, and the aroma of pasta and coffee filled the room, making my stomach growl even more. I wanted to devour it all.

He watched me with a smile as I took a bite of the pasta, and I gave him a thumbs-up to say it was delicious.

Then, I looked up and asked, "Where did you go last night from Sara's place?"

He coughed; the coffee stuck in his throat. Clearing his throat, he said, "I went early in the morning. I didn't want to cause any trouble. I didn't want anyone to see me, especially since I had to sneak into Sara's house like a thief, climbing the rain pipe. So, I went when it was still dark. But why are you asking?"

"You could have woken me up at least."

"You were asleep. How could I wake you up? You looked like an angel while you slept."

I grabbed a spoonful of pasta and said, "That was really romantic. But do you know what I had to hear from Sara?"

Then I told him everything that happened with me and Sara at her house, at the office, and even what happened with the HR at my company. I also told him about receiving a one-month notice from work.

He listened carefully, as always. It was his best habit - he was a great listener. Whenever I spoke, he paid full attention, his ears wide open.

"It's really sad," he said, his voice calm. "But don't worry about the job. You're great at coding. You'll find something even better."

"Yeah," I replied, enjoying my pasta and coffee.

"But Sara shouldn't have acted like that. She should treat you better, especially since you're her best friend."

"Hmmm."

"You feel bad for her, don't you?"

"Yeah."

"If you want, I can talk to her. I'll make our relationship clear."

"No."

Chirag seemed like he wanted to say something, but I interrupted him. "You don't understand, baby. Ever since I told her about you, her attitude completely changed. She became so jealous of me, of us, of our relationship. Don't talk to that bitch. She doesn't care about you. She'll only insult you. And if she does, no one on Earth will be able to protect her from me." My voice was steady, firm, and clear.

Chirag pulled me into a hug and kissed my forehead. I set aside the dish, having finished my meal. I leaned into his arms, wanting to spend the rest of the night there. He gently brushed my hair, and I felt myself drift off to sleep, the cool breeze from the balcony softly caressing my skin. As the night slowly came to an end, I was completely lost in his embrace.

CHAPTER XV

15th October, Thursday.

The sunlight hit my balcony, waking me up. It was already afternoon. How long had I been sleeping? Had I been drugged somehow to stay asleep that long? No, probably not. It didn't matter—I felt no guilt. That long sleep had recharged me like pressing a restart button. Besides, it wasn't as if I needed to wake up early; the days of rushing to the office and diving into code were over.

Bigger problems waited for me now—problems like Raj Reddy and his company. Still lying in bed, I replayed yesterday's events in my mind. The memory of being trapped in Raj's world hadn't faded one bit. I wondered what Sara was up to at work. She was probably doing just fine without me, maybe even happier. Just then, my phone buzzed beside me on the bed.

It was a call from the office—HR's landline number. I saw it, and I cursed under my breath, "Damn you, Kamini Duggal." She was the HR manager, and I hated her. I didn't pick up. The phone went silent, but after a couple of seconds, a message popped up on my screen. It was from her: "You are supposed to report to the office at 9:15. Come here and report to me immediately."

I rolled my eyes. "Fuck off," I muttered.

I knew exactly why she was calling. There were several projects at the office that used Python, and without me, no one else could handle them. I was the expert, the only one who could do it right. I couldn't help but feel a little proud of that. It was my edge, the one thing that set me apart.

Suddenly, I realized something—I hadn't seen Chirag since I'd woken up. Lying in bed, too lazy to move, I sniffed the air like a curious dog, trying to catch any hint of his presence in the flat. But no, he wasn't there. Sure, Chirag wasn't my husband, hovering around to follow my every order, but still—where was he?

A strange feeling churned in my stomach. Could he have gone to Raj's place? Oh no! He'd promised me he wouldn't. But what if he broke his promise while I was asleep? I remembered how angry he looked when I told him everything about Raj and his company. His face had turned red as I spoke, rage building with every word. He'd definitely gone there.

Oh, my God! No, Chirag. No, baby! My head was throbbing, and I felt dizzy. What if Raj had taken Chirag and made him his prisoner? What if Chirag was trapped, just like I was last night in that factory? What could I do now?

I couldn't go to the police—Chirag had warned me against it. Besides, I couldn't be sure the police would actually help; some of them worked for Raj, like Sub-Inspector Vijay.

I was out of options. Was there anyone else who could help? Maybe Sara—her father was a top criminal lawyer with connections all over the city. But Sara and I... we were done. That door was closed, and I knew she wouldn't help me.

Oh, then what happened? I couldn't believe it—Chirag was stuck with those thugs and criminals. I couldn't just sit here doing nothing. I had to go for him. I jumped out of bed and rushed to the bathroom, quickly splashing water on my face. I knew I had to move fast.

As I walked back to the room from the washroom, the warm scent of ginger-mint black coffee filled the air. Feeling a sudden burst of joy, I spun around and called out, "Chirag!" There he was, stepping out of the kitchen, carrying a tray with two black coffees and a sandwich.

"Where were you?" I asked, smiling.

"I was in the kitchen," he replied.

He placed the tray on the bed, smiling at me. I hugged him, feeling grateful. Having Chirag in my life felt like a blessing from God. With him by my side, I was ready to take on anything.

"What's wrong?" he asked.

"I thought... maybe you'd left me for Raj," I whispered.

He looked at me softly and said, "How could I leave? You made me promise that if I ever did, you'd jump from this balcony. I'd never want to see that happen."

His words were gentle, like a soft breeze brushing past my ear. "Now, don't overthink," he murmured. "Come on, let's enjoy our coffee and sandwich."

I didn't want to admit how badly I needed this coffee. I picked up the cup and took a sip, letting the warmth settle.

"So, what have you decided?" he asked.

"Decided? About what?"

"About dealing with Raj and his company."

I shook my head. "I haven't decided anything. I don't know," I looked up and added, "I just don't want you going near him." I was certain. No way was I letting Chirag get involved with Raj.

"So, how long will you keep hiding here?" he asked. "Raj's men are probably keeping a close watch on your flat."

I said nothing, focusing on my coffee and sandwich. As I ate, I noticed him watching me, that familiar warmth in his brown eyes.

"You're such a child," he said, gently brushing his hand over my cheek. I leaned my head on his chest, a piece of sandwich still in my mouth, and he stroked my hair softly.

"Rishika..."

"Hmm?"

"Why don't we just get away from here?"

"Why not?" I saw the spark in his eyes; he had a plan. "It's a great idea. I have nothing left in this city for me. I could leave behind Raj and Sara, the coding job, this tech city, and all the meaningless stuff. Just leave it all behind and escape."

"But where would we go?"

"Mumbai?" I suggested. "You've been there, so you'd know people. We could start fresh there." I didn't say it, but in my mind, I imagined us getting married and starting a whole new life together.

"But Rishika, a smaller town, would be safer for us. They could find us easily in Mumbai... and honestly, I'm tired of big cities. All these high-rises, the crowded streets—I've had enough. I just want to disappear somewhere quiet, away from the noise of Bengaluru."

"That's great. I felt the same way," I said. "I'm with you, but where will we go?"

"We'll go to Kovalam," he replied, his voice warm and certain. "It's a beautiful coastal town in Kerala. We'll live in a traditional Kerala-style house and stay there forever, peaceful and quiet," His eyes seemed to look right into the future, seeing it all.

"Have you stayed there?" I cut him off from dreaming about living in Kovalam. I continued, "Your eyes tell me that right now you are lost in the beauty of Kovalam and can see our future there."

He spoke softly as he could still feel the sand between his toes. "Kovalam was beautiful," he murmured.

"The sand stretched on and on, and the waves sparkled in the sunlight. Tall coconut trees lined the beach, swaying gently with the breeze. The lighthouse stood proudly like an old friend watching over the shore. It was so peaceful. It felt like we could stay there forever, just us, far away from everything."

He paused, smiling. "I once went there with my friends from Mumbai, and I loved it."

"Then it's decided—we'll stay in Kovalam," I said, hugging him tightly. It was finally happening; we were leaving the city behind.

We lay on the bed, arms around each other, looking up pictures and videos of Kovalam on my phone—watching vlogs, reading guides, taking in every bit of beauty we could find.

At that moment, the world felt far away, and only the promise of Kovalam mattered.

Time slipped by in his arms, and before I knew it, evening had come. I looked out from the balcony, watching the city lights glow below.

I stretched my arms wide as I got out of bed. Standing by the balcony, I looked out at the beautiful city of Bengaluru. "We've been cooped up here all day," I said, feeling restless. "I'm bored. Let's go for a walk."

"Yeah, great idea," he replied, "But we should take care—not to get caught by Raj's men."

• • •

We had been walking hand in hand that evening, feeling happy and crying at the same time. We savored the delicious South Indian street food because I was hungry. The cool breeze, the city lights, and the people around us made everything feel surreal. As I walked, I thought about how soon I would be leaving this city. No more seeing Sara, no more coding at Zenith Networks, no more of the usual stuff. Just Chirag, me, and Kovalam.

I got lost in thoughts about Kovalam and didn't realize where Chirag had gone. He was standing a few steps behind me, outside the Gym—Garden City Fitness Center.

I walked over to him, laughing, and said, "So, you skipped your gym session today and want to do it now?"

"Oh, no, dear," he replied.

"Well, this is your gym, isn't it? You disappear every morning from your flat, and I keep seeing a lock hanging on your door."

"Ah, but I came here for another reason," he said, his voice dropping lower.

"What reason?" I asked, confused.

"This gym has a locker facility for its members," he replied.

"So?" I raised an eyebrow.

"I have something in the locker that belongs to me," he said, looking away.

"Well, let's go get your thing then," I said, ready to follow.

He hesitated. "Will you... want to come with me?"

"Why not? You don't want me there?" I asked, sensing something strange.

He flushed red, looking like he was hiding something. "Yeah, baby, this gym is for men only. It might be awkward if you come along."

I could see the unease on his face, and it made me even more curious. What was he trying to keep from me?

"I'll come with you. Don't worry; no guy in the gym will try anything. I trust your muscles and the testosterone in your blood," I said with a teasing laugh, hoping to ease his tension.

Chirag had no choice but to nod. We walked into the gym. Inside, through the big glass walls, I could see many guys working out. Chirag was right—they were all staring at me. Some of them even started showing off, trying to get my attention. We made our way to the locker area, passing by the glass walls.

Chirag opened his locker, which was at his height, using a key he took from his jeans pocket. I peered inside. There were towels and other items, but what caught my eye was a black backpack that looked heavy.

Curious, I asked, "What's in the backpack?"

"Just some guy's stuff," Chirag said. Then he opened one of the zips. I couldn't see inside, but when he pulled something out, I froze in shock.

It was a gun.

CHAPTER XVI

He pulled the gun out of his backpack, glancing around suspiciously. Then, with a quick motion, he tucked it into his waist, hiding it beneath his T-shirt.

"What's that, Chirag?" I asked, confused.

"It's a gun—a 9mm," he replied.

"What?" I was even more puzzled.

"Let's go," Chirag said hurriedly, locking the locker with his keys and pulling me along.

My mind was racing with questions. I wanted answers, but Chirag was in a rush. He dragged me out of the gym. Once we were outside, he didn't seem like he wanted to stop, but I couldn't let it go. I needed to know. So, I stopped us in a quiet, empty spot, far from the gym and the road.

"What is going on, Chirag?" I asked, my voice urgent.

He looked at me and said, "It's a gun, dear. You can't see it?"

"I can see it, but why do you have it?" I pressed.

"Rishika, it's for our safety from Raj and his goons," he replied.

I sighed deeply. He was right. Chirag had kept the gun in the gym locker, which is why the police hadn't found it during the raid in our neighborhood. That raid had happened because of a phone call I made to the police, a call made in a moment of misunderstanding with Chirag.

"Do you know how to shoot a gun?" he asked.

"No, why should I know?" I replied.

"It's for our safety, dear. I'll teach you. It's simple."

"I don't want to learn," I said. Why should I need to know how to shoot a gun?

"Please, learn. The future might not be safe for us," he said, his voice carrying a strange tone that made me agree to learn.

We walked down the empty street, heading to a place where there were no houses, no shops—just trees and barren land. It felt like we were the only ones in the world.

Chirag carefully pulled out a gun, its cold metal shining faintly in the dim light. He handed it to me, and as his fingers brushed mine, a jolt of adrenaline rushed through me. "This," he said in a low voice, "is the safety lock. Don't forget it. And here's the cartridge—always check it before you aim."

I nodded, trying to calm my racing heart as I listened closely to every word. He moved behind me, his breath warm against my neck. The gun felt heavy in my hands, but I gripped it tightly.

"Relax," he whispered. "Control it. Aim with precision."

His voice was steady, but the intensity in his eyes pushed me to focus harder. I held the gun, recalling every detail he'd taught me. "Now, pull the trigger gently, like you're ready to strike."

I took a deep breath, my finger on the cold metal. My mind sharpened as I aimed. Time seemed to slow as I focused on the target ahead.

Then, the first shot broke the silence. It echoed in my ears like a challenge.

"I can't do it," I said in a defeated tone.

"You can do it," he persuaded me to learn gun shooting.

"Didn't you see how I felt shocked by gunfire?"

"It happens the first time, but... you will learn."

He persisted with me, and I tried again. Then I tried once more. After five shots, my fear of gun shooting disappeared, and I was enjoying it.

Only then did my phone buzz. I saw it—an unknown number. Chirag saw me from afar; I showed him the phone buzzing, displaying an unknown number.

"Pick up and put on the speaker," he said, coming near me.

I handed the gun to him, picked up the call, and put the phone on speaker.

It was Raj. My heart sank. His harsh voice echoed in the silence of the place like the gunshot that I had heard earlier.

"Hello, you liar, sweetie! Where are you, darling, right now? You are smarter than I imagined. I'm wondering how you could move from your flat. I think I need better men. They are all bastards; don't do a single and simple work properly," he said.

"Why do you call me?"

"Listen, girl, don't try my patience." Then suddenly, he screamed on the call, "You told me everything was bullshit. All of it was bullshit. You think I am a fool."

"Whatever you want to say, say it clearly," I said. With Chirag standing beside me, I got the courage to talk to Raj confidently.

"Listen, then. You told me that you got money from a guy named J.K. Right?"

"Right."

"I found that J.K."

Oh, God. Please, Raj, I didn't find J.K.—my colleague. I looked into Chirag's brown eyes. They were red with anger.

Raj said as if he was mocking me, "He is your colleague, isn't he?"

I replied by controlling my emotions, "No."

"Don't lie to me."

"I don't lie. The guy who gave me money named J.K. that is a different one who is my colleague."

"Lie. Lie. Lie," he shouted on the phone. "You never know any other J.K."

Chirag whispered to me that I spoke the truth to Raj so that J.K. wouldn't suffer for my lie.

"Are you dead in there?" Raj said.

"I'm here."

"Listen, you cheating girl. You lied to me, you named J.K., and J.K. had to suffer throughout the day," he said in an angry tone.

"What did you do with J.K.?" I wanted to know about J.K., my colleague. Though I was not connected to J.K. so much, I didn't feel good if someone suffered because of me.

"My men dragged J.K. from the office. They beat him up throughout the day and asked for the money that he was supposed to give you. My men tortured him a lot. But every time, he said the same line, 'he had no connection with you and the money, he had not given any job offer to you, and he is not going to start any start-up. It was all a lie which you told me earlier." He was yelling on the phone.

I was full of emotions, and tears came out for J.K., an innocent guy who suffered for me without any reason.

I yelled on the phone, "You know you are a monster!"

Raj was laughing like mad. He said, "Yeah, baby, I am a monster when someone steals my money. I love to become a monster. But you have not seen my true monster face yet."

"You have beaten up an innocent guy—J.K."

"That was because of you."

"When I told you that I got money from the J.K., I was not talking about my colleague J.K. He was someone else," I said, my voice shaking.

"Again, you are lying. You know you are a bitch—damn bitch. Just return my money, girl; otherwise, I will take the skin off your body. I will smash your face." He said as if he was pissing on me.

Before I could speak, Chirag was ready to answer Raj, but I stopped him. I didn't want to show Chirag. But he was looking very angry. His shoulders were up and down, and his chest moved fast with heavy breath.

I said to Raj in a calm voice, as I believed that heating up an argument with Raj could bring many bad consequences for J.K., "Listen, J.K. is not in Bengaluru; he is in Delhi, and when he returns, I will come to you with J.K., till then wait and please let my colleague J.K. go out of your place. He has suffered a lot because of a misunderstanding."

"Oh, now you feel love for your colleague J.K. But I am not in the mood of letting him go out of my place until you come here with my money," he said in a sharp voice.

My eyes met with Chirag's. He nodded as he had something on his mind.

"Okay, I agree."

"That's right, my girl, so come fast because my men are going to plow J.K.'s nails one by one from his fingers," he laughed and continued, "And don't try to do nonsense like calling the police because this will have bad consequences for you and your ally in the crime." He hung up the phone.

In that silence of the night, we stood shocked.

Chirag said in a hurry, "Rishika, you go to the flat; I will go for those bastards."

"No, Chirag. I will go. It's my matter," I said firmly.

"Your matter? Rishika, try to understand all this begins with the money I gave you. First, Ramesh took it wrongly, and now his brother Raj, who killed his own brother, Ramesh, wants you to frame him before the police. Let me go to his place; I will talk to them; I will offer them to keep me behind bars for the crime which I didn't do, but let you go out of all this," he said, his brown eyes sparkled.

"What are you saying, Chirag? Don't be silly. If the situation comes to going behind bars, then I will go, not you." I touched his chin with love in my eyes.

Without saying a word, he hugged me. I was in the world's most peaceful place—in his arms. Forget the world—Raj and all. If Raj had no J.K., then I would tell Chirag to leave this city and let's go to Kovalam.

Then he pulled away and said, "Rishika, if you love me, let me go."

I understood that Chirag had made up his mind.

"I have a better idea," I said.

"What?"

"We both go to Raj's place. But first, I enter; you will follow me to enter without being noticed by any of Raj's guards."

It looked like Chirag had no big problems with this idea, but he had some fear to follow that idea; his face showed that. He said, "It's risky."

"What risk when you would also be there."

Chirag nodded at the idea. He said while giving the gun to me, "Better to keep the gun with you."

"But they will hear it from me."

"Don't be silly, just hide it in your clothes. I guessed that Raj and his men would not check you for the gun. They think of you as a simple tech girl expert in coding, not an expert in firing bullets. They will not think in their dreams that you are a gun girl."

"But what about you? I suppose that you will carry the gun and protect us from those monsters," I said.

Chirag said, "Don't worry about me. My hands are enough for them." Chirag looked at his hands and I looked at his biceps that were just as big and strong as my thigh.

We headed to Raj's place. I felt like an actor from an action thriller movie, and the climax was approaching as we would meet Raj and his company.

• • •

I was in that abandoned factory once again, where I was being kept by Raj's goons. That thought sent shivers down my spine.

As Chirag told me, I observed everything carefully. Raj was sitting on a sofa-like chair at the center of the main hall of the factory. Police SI Vijay was standing near him as if he were not a policeman but Raj's guard.

I saw six of Raj's men standing here and there. They all looked like criminals with dark skin. They looked so dangerous. They had no arms; I meant I saw no arms in their hands; if they were there, I didn't know. Chirag was right; they didn't check me.

To them, I was only a tech girl into coding, not fighting. To them, I liked to watch only romantic movies, not action movies. I could feel the iron of the gun, which was tucked on my waist under my hoodie.

And then, I noticed J.K. as I took more steps ahead, crossing many old and broken machines and machine parts.

He sat slumped in the corner of the hall, his body tied tightly with thick ropes that dug into his bruised skin. His face was swollen and smeared with blood, and cuts ran across his cheeks and forehead. His clothes were torn and stained, clinging to his battered body. He could barely keep his eyes open. The goons had done their job brutally. He could see into my eyes with a lot of effort.

"Please..." he whispered hoarsely, his voice barely audible, begging for mercy from anyone who might hear. His hands twisted weakly against the ropes, but they wouldn't budge.

144

CHAPTER XVII

"Look, I'm here now. Let J.K. go," I said firmly, though my heart ached to see J.K.'s terrible state.

For a moment, there was complete silence. Then Raj burst into loud laughter. Vijay joined in, their laughter echoing as if it were the punchline of some cruel joke. Letting J.K. go? To them, it was hilarious.

Vijay smirked, his eyes cold as he said, "I don't get you. You say J.K. has nothing to do with your money or any deal with us. So why do you care about him? Whether he lives or dies shouldn't matter to you."

He was mocking me, trying to break me down, but I held on. "It's true," I said, keeping my voice steady despite the fear creeping in. "J.K. has nothing to do with me or the money. He doesn't know anything. I care about him as a human being—something you wouldn't understand. Please, I'm begging you... let him go."

And yes, I begged. For J.K.'s life, I begged them.

"Girl! Don't test my patience. I told you on the call that J.K. would only be free if you brought my money. So, where is it?" Raj's voice thundered, echoing through the abandoned factory. The sound startled a flock of pigeons, which fluttered away from their perch high up in the dark corners of the ceiling.

Before I could explain, Vijay sneered, his voice dripping with malice. "Sir, she came empty-handed. Strolling in here like it's some park, acting all casual. Just say the word, and I'll make her talk about the money."

A chill ran down my spine. My hands trembled as I watched Vijay's cold gaze meet Raj's. Raj gave a curt nod, and Vijay turned toward me, his steps slow and deliberate. My heart sank, pounding so loudly I thought they might hear it. My legs felt frozen, my back numb with fear.

Vijay stepped closer, his voice cold and menacing. "Baby, last time when you were here, we treated you with care. But this time, there's no mercy. You'll face the consequences unless you tell us where the money is."

As he approached, I instinctively stepped back, but he was faster. Grabbing a fistful of my hair, he yanked me forward and slammed me onto the floor. Pain shot through my scalp as if he thought I was some lifeless object he could drag around. Tears welled up in my eyes, spilling over as the sting became unbearable.

Leaning in close, Vijay hissed, "Tell me where the money is! Don't even try lying. I've seen through your games. That 'J.K. theory' you cooked up? Total nonsense. You don't have a friend who gave you the money. It was all you—you robbed CredZone, and you killed Ramesh, Sir. Admit it! Tell me I'm right."

His words sliced through the air, each one sharper than the last. My mind raced, the fear and pain twisting together into a chaotic storm.

I was stunned by everything Vijay said. It was shocking to realize that Chirag had been right all along. These people had framed me for crimes I hadn't committed. The only relief was that they didn't know about Chirag. At least he wasn't dragged into this mess as my so-called partner in crime.

Vijay's bloodshot eyes burned with rage, and his voice was cold as steel. "Tell me the truth. If you don't, you won't leave this factory alive. Only your corpse will walk out of here."

He yanked my hair, sending a sharp pain through my scalp. I winced but managed to speak, my voice trembling. "I swear, I didn't do anything you're accusing me of. I didn't rob CredZone, and I didn't kill Ramesh Reddy."

Raj's voice cut through the tension, filled with anger. "Then tell us the name of the bastard—your partner in crime!" he shouted from across the room.

I was trapped, surrounded by their fury, with no way out.

I struggled to free myself from Vijay's grip, but it was no use. His hand clutched tightly to my hair, refusing to let go.

"I don't have any partner in crime," I said, my voice trembling. "I only gave the money to your brother, Ramesh. It was from a friend."

Vijay sneered his face inches from mine. "And that friend—let me guess—is J.K.? Not this J.K. we have locked up, but some *other* J.K., right?" With those words, he shoved my face hard against the cold, unforgiving floor. "Isn't that the truth, girl?"

I winced as pain shot through my face. "Yes," I whispered, barely able to speak.

That one word ignited his rage. Vijay grabbed my face, his fingers digging into my skin, and slapped me so hard that my vision blurred.

The first slap wasn't the end. It was just the beginning.

Thwack! Thwack!

One after another, the sound of his palm meeting my face echoed in the room, each strike stinging more than the last.

The sound of Vijay's slap echoed through the hall, sharp and unforgiving. My cheek stung, and I felt a burning cut open on my face. Blood trickled from my split lip, warm and metallic. Before I could react, his fist crashed into my left eye, and the world blurred as pain exploded in my head.

I stumbled, trying to steady myself, but he grabbed me by the neck, his grip crushing and dehumanizing. I felt small, like a rag doll in his hands. Shame and anger twisted inside me, but I had no strength to fight back.

Then, out of the corner of my eye, I spotted something strange—Chirag, perched silently on the iron beam above us, watching like a shadow in the dim light.

Before I could process it, Vijay's boot collided with my chest, sending me flying. I hit the ground hard, landing at Raj's feet. The force of the fall jarred something loose—the gun, hidden under my clothes, tumbled out and clattered onto the floor.

The room seemed to freeze for a moment, the air thick with tension. Everyone's eyes were on the weapon. My secret was out, and the game had just changed.

Raj and his men froze in shock when they saw the gun in my hand. Just as they were about to react, Chirag appeared out of nowhere. No one saw him coming, and his sudden arrival left everyone stunned. Without wasting a second, Chirag lunged forward, grabbing the gun and pressing it firmly against Raj's neck.

Now, Raj was at Chirag's mercy.

"Don't move, or your boss is done for!" Chirag roared, his voice echoing like a lion's growl.

Vijay, standing nearby, panicked. His hand moved subtly toward the gun tucked in his waistband, trying to pull off a quick move. But Chirag was faster. A shot rang out, and Vijay collapsed to the ground, clutching his leg and screaming in agony. Blood pooled beneath him as he writhed in pain, his face twisted in fear and desperation.

Raj's fury burned in his eyes, but he couldn't do anything. I stepped closer to Chirag, my heart pounding as I tried to process the chaos unraveling in front of me.

Raj's voice trembled with fear as he said, "You can leave. I don't want your money." His words seemed sincere, but his fingers told a different story. He subtly gestured to his men, signaling them to act.

The men, who had been standing still like statues, suddenly came to life. One of them pulled a knife from his pocket and hurled it straight at Chirag. But Chirag was faster. His sharp eyes caught the gleaming blade flying toward him.

In a swift move, Chirag dodged the knife. He didn't just save himself — he saved me too. Without wasting a second, he pulled out his gun and fired. The bullet hit the man square in the forehead, dropping him to the ground, lifeless.

In the very next second, Chirag turned the gun toward Raj and pressed it against his neck. Raj froze, unable to even flinch. He didn't have a moment to react.

I stood frozen, staring at Chirag in disbelief. His eyes burned red with rage, and for the first time, I couldn't bear to meet his gaze.

Chirag shouted at Raj, "Tell your men to free J.K.! Let him go right now!"

I turned to look at J.K. He was tied up with ropes, a prisoner of Raj. His head hung to the side, his face pale with pain. Blood stained his clothes. His eyes were shut tight. My chest tightened with guilt. J.K. was in this situation because of me. If anything happened to him, I'd never forgive myself.

Raj looked like he was about to follow Chirag's orders, but then something unexpected happened. Vijay, who was crying out in pain after Chirag shot him in the leg, suddenly pulled a gun from his waistband. His hands were shaking, but his aim was steady as he pointed the gun at J.K.

"No!" I screamed, but it was too late. Vijay fired.

The gunshot echoed in the room, and J.K. fell limp. He was gone.

Vijay laughed like a maniac, his face twisted with pain and madness, blood pouring from his injured leg. "See? Your friend is dead!" he taunted, his voice sharp and cruel.

Before I could react, Chirag raised his gun. Bang! Bang!

The first bullet shattered Vijay's shoulder, sending him stumbling backward. The second hit him in the heart. Vijay collapsed to the floor, lifeless, his laughter silenced forever.

The room fell quiet, except for the pounding of my heart and the distant echo of the gunshots.

I ran toward J.K. Vijay had fired the bullet, and it struck J.K. right in the forehead, shattering his skull. Blood gushed out like a fountain, staining everything around. My stomach churned at the horrifying sight, and I couldn't bear it. I staggered to a corner of the hall and started vomiting.

Suddenly, I felt a soft touch on my back. It was Chirag. His hand rested gently, trying to comfort me. I turned to look into his eyes, my own brimming with pain and guilt. In a trembling voice, I said, "We couldn't save J.K. He's dead because of me."

Chirag's voice was steady, but his eyes showed the same grief. "Don't blame yourself," he said firmly. "You didn't do anything wrong. J.K. is dead because of those bastards."

Bang! Bang! Bang!

The sound of gunfire erupted, cutting through the moment. Raj and his men were firing at us. My heart stopped for a second, but Chirag acted fast. He grabbed me and jumped with me behind a metal shed, its rusted surface our only shield in the abandoned chemical factory. Bullets rained down, clanging loudly against the iron.

We were safe, for now. My hands trembled, and fear coursed through me. For a moment, I thought it was the end. We were going to die here, and our plan to escape to Kovalam would never happen.

I looked at Chirag's face. There was no fear. His eyes sparkled with excitement as if he had been waiting for this exact moment. Suddenly, the sound of bullets slowed down. The chaos seemed to pause, and in that instant, Chirag stood up and fired back.

He moved quickly, shooting at the attackers while staying behind cover. He signaled me to stay under the iron shed and not to move. I watched him dodging bullets and shifting positions to keep firing. He didn't stop, and I couldn't look away. Fear gripped me—what if a bullet hit him? What if he... didn't make it?

That thought drained every bit of strength from me. My head spun, my vision blurred, and my knees gave out.

"Rishika! Rishika! Open your eyes!"

When I opened my eyes, I was in Chirag's strong arms. His voice was firm yet gentle.

"Are you okay?" he asked.

"Yes, I think so," I whispered.

"Are you done?" I asked, my voice shaking.

"Yes," he replied, a spark of joy in his eyes. He helped me stand, steadying me. As I looked around, the reality of what had just happened sank in.

The place was eerily silent. The sharp smell of gunpowder hung in the air, a reminder of the recent gunshots that had echoed through the building. I walked cautiously with Chirag, my heart pounding.

Bodies lay scattered on the floor—Raj's men, lifeless and bloodied. My eyes landed on Raj himself. His body was drenched in blood, four bullets clearly lodged in his chest. His lifeless eyes were wide open, almost as if they were staring straight at me. A shiver ran down my spine.

I turned to Chirag, startled. He met my gaze and said, "Now, you don't need to worry. All your problems are lying dead right here."

Before I could respond, the sound of police sirens blared in the distance, growing louder with every second. Chirag's face hardened with frustration.

"Rishika, move! We need to leave. The police are coming!" he urged, his voice sharp.

I stood my ground and replied firmly, "So what, Chirag? We've done nothing wrong. We can explain everything to the police."

Chirag's irritation was clear. "And when they ask us about the bodies, what will we say?" he shot back, his voice laced with tension.

"We'll just say it was all in self-defense," I said, trying to steady my trembling voice.

"Don't be stupid, Rishika!" Chirag snapped, his anger cutting through the tension. It was the first time I had ever seen him so irritated, and it unsettled me. His eyes burned with frustration as he continued, "Look around! There's blood everywhere. Half a dozen people are dead, and we're the only ones left standing. And don't forget—one of them is a cop, Vijay. Without evidence to back us up, the police won't believe a word we say. They'll bombard us with questions and then lock us up."

He paused, his chest heaving, before adding quietly, "You need to leave. I'll stay and face whatever comes. This mess is my fault, and I'll take the blame. Just go before the police arrive."

"No, Chirag," I said firmly, my heart pounding in my chest. "Don't you dare suggest something like that? I can't live knowing you're behind bars because of this." I took a deep breath and made up my mind. "You're right – we can't get involved with the police. We're done here. Let's leave now."

Chirag hesitated but finally nodded. "Alright, but we move fast—through the back exit."

CHAPTER XVIII

16th October, Friday.

I woke up late—so late that the sun was already shining directly onto my balcony. Actually, I only opened my eyes when the sun's rays warmed my bed, and by then, it was almost noon. Even after waking up, I felt sluggish and heavy with laziness.

I needed coffee—strong, black coffee—and that meant I needed Chirag.

"This isn't good, Rishika," I muttered to myself. "You're getting way too dependent on Chirag." But I couldn't help it. He made the best black coffee with a twist of ginger and mint, or so I thought.

"Chirag!" I called out, my voice echoing through the flat. Silence. No answer. That meant he wasn't here. Annoyed, I reached for my phone to call him.

That's when it hit me—one terrible memory from last night. My phone was dead, completely useless. The screen had shattered when it slipped from my hand during the chaos.

It happened as Chirag and I scrambled over the ten-foot-high boundary wall of the factory, desperate to escape the police.

Oh, last night was terrifying!

Even now, I could see flashes of what happened—the fight, the gunshot, the blood, the lifeless bodies. It all came rushing back, haunting me like a nightmare I couldn't escape. Sleep didn't come easily, not after returning from Raj's place. That abandoned factory was now burned into my memory.

Back in my flat, even with Chirag by my side, fear gripped me tightly. He tried to comfort me, running his fingers gently through my hair. It was soothing, but deep down, I couldn't shake off the unease. Chirag's behavior at Raj's place—what he did and how he acted—sent a chill through me. Who was this man I thought I knew so well?

Eventually, exhaustion pulled me under, and I drifted off in Chirag's arms. His presence felt like the only anchor keeping me from falling apart.

But now, as I woke up, a new fear crept in. Where was he? My arms searched the empty space beside me, and I called out, my voice trembling, "Chirag?"

I heard footsteps near the main door. The soft creak of it opening and closing echoed through the room. A few moments later, he stood in front of me, smiling as he always did.

"Where were you? And where's my coffee?" I asked, pretending to be angry. I even added a dramatic flair, acting like a demanding wife who expected her every wish to be fulfilled.

"In just a moment, dear," Chirag replied with his usual calmness and disappeared into the kitchen.

I grabbed my broken phone and started taking pretend selfies while lying on the bed, striking random poses. If the phone had been working, I would have been capturing real selfies. But since it wasn't, I simply imagined the clicks. After what felt like a dozen pretend shots, Chirag returned, holding two mugs of coffee.

"What are you doing? Your phone doesn't even work. How are you taking selfies?" he asked, amused.

Still posing, I replied with a smirk, "Old habits die hard, dear."

"Give me your phone. I'll get it repaired by this evening," he said, reaching out.

I handed it over, chuckling. It was moments like these that made life feel normal – or at least close to it.

I took a cup of coffee, drawn by its rich aroma. As I sipped, I glanced over at Chirag. He stood by the balcony, staring out at the city we were about to leave behind.

"Baby," I called softly.

He turned, shifting his gaze from the twinkling skyline to me. "Yeah, baby?" he asked with a small smile.

"Are we really leaving tonight?" I asked, trying to hide the nervous edge in my voice.

"Yes," he nodded. "The train tickets are confirmed for late tonight. You know that." His smile was calm, almost reassuring.

But I wasn't calm. That night, I lay awake, haunted by memories of the horrifying events at the factory. The images wouldn't let me rest. I couldn't stay in this city any longer—it felt like the walls were closing in.

I had begged Chirag to leave Bengaluru with me and head to Kovalam, just as we had planned before. He didn't argue. He simply opened my laptop, booked the tickets, and promised we'd leave as soon as possible.

Now, as I stared at the laptop, a different thought crept into my mind. The news. The factory. What were the police saying about it? Did they have any suspects? I needed to know.

The answers were just a click away. And yet, I hesitated.

I jumped out of bed and grabbed my laptop from the desk nearby. My hands trembled as I opened it, my mind racing.

Chirag, sitting across the room with his coffee, took a sip and asked casually, "What are you doing?"

"I want to check the news," I said, logging into the browser. My voice was sharper than I intended. "What's happening now? Did the police find anything about what happened at the factory last night?"

Before I could load the page, Chirag stepped forward and slammed the laptop shut. The sound made me flinch.

"What are you doing?" I asked, frowning at him.

He shook his head, his brown eyes filled with worry. "Why are you digging into this again? Don't you remember what you went through last night? Don't bring that trauma back. Just... stop thinking about it. Act like we weren't even there. Like none of it happened."

His words hung in the air, heavy and loaded with fear. I couldn't tell if he was more concerned about me—or about the truth coming out.

I knew Chirag was right. Seeing the news and pictures again would make my head feel like it would explode. But I still said, "You're right, Chirag. But we need to know what the police are thinking about the killers. What are the news channels saying about it?"

Chirag's voice had a hint of anger as he replied, "Let me tell you something. The police are chasing the criminals who killed Raj, the so-called 'kind money lender' of the city. Vijay, the sub-inspector, and his security guards. According to them, these men were 'great people' who didn't deserve to die. They think the killers should be locked away for life."

He stopped for a moment as if trying to calm himself, then continued, his voice more intense. "This is what's wrong with this country! Raj was no saint. He was a big businessman running a money-laundering racket under the pretense of helping the poor. And Vijay? The 'honest cop' in police records? He's the same man who tortured you and tried to frame you for crimes you didn't commit."

Chirag's breathing grew heavier, his chest rising and falling in anger. His fists clenched tightly as he added, "And now, the police are after *us*—the real victims of monsters like Raj and Vijay."

His words hung in the air, thick with frustration and pain, as I watched him struggle to contain his rage.

I placed my hand gently on his shoulder. After a moment, he seemed calmer. Then he reached out, held my hand, and pulled me into his broad chest.

It was our last day in the city, and I wanted to make the most of it. I decided we should spend the day walking through the streets, exploring every corner, arm in arm, and reliving the memories we had made here. Chirag thought it was a brilliant idea and agreed instantly.

We stepped out of the flat together, ready to bid farewell to the city that had been my home for the past four years. But first, I had to get my phone fixed. At the repair shop, the shopkeeper told me the phone wouldn't be ready until night. That was fine – I'd have the entire day with Chirag and no distractions. The only downside was that I couldn't take selfies to capture these last precious moments. But maybe that made it even more special.

I felt a strange mix of happiness and sadness as I stood at the edge of my life in Bengaluru, ready to leave it behind. This city had been more than just a place—it had been a part of me. Bengaluru gave me so much, yet it also took so much in return.

It gave me Chirag, the love of my life, the one who made my heart feel alive again. It gave me a chance to start over, to leave my past behind and step into a new chapter—a life waiting for me in the serene beauty of Kovalam, Kerala.

But as I prepared to say goodbye, I wondered, *Would I miss this city?* The maddening traffic that seemed endless? The towering skyscrapers that touched the clouds? The unique scent of Bengaluru—a mix of its lush lakes and gardens with the hum of technology from its bustling IT hub?

Leaving wasn't just about packing bags; it was about leaving a piece of myself behind. The thought lingered, as bittersweet as the memories this city had etched in my soul.

First, I went to Zenith Networks. No, I didn't go inside my old office. I just stood on the road in front of the building. Zenith Networks was on the fifth floor, and I imagined the people there working like robots—writing code, attending endless meetings, chasing targets like machines. Bla bla bla.

I knew it was crazy, but I didn't care. Standing there on that road, I raised both my middle fingers toward the building. My heart was pounding, and tears filled my eyes. That place had stolen so many sleepless nights from me—nights when I could have rested like the dead.

But at that moment, I didn't cry because I was sad. I cried because I felt free. I showed them my middle fingers with tears streaming down my face, and for the first time, I felt truly happy.

We explored more places in the city, and I couldn't stop talking. I told Chirag all about the places that held special memories for me. Each spot made me relive those moments, celebrating them one last time before leaving the city. But as the reality of leaving sank in, my chest felt heavy, and my throat tightened with emotion.

Chirag noticed my feelings without me saying a word. He smiled and said, "Let's go to Cyrus' Corner."

His suggestion lit up something inside me. How could I forget Cyrus's Corner? It was a place we both cherished, filled with shared memories. Without another thought, we went there.

The evening air was cool, and couples were beginning to gather. We found our favorite spot, the corner seat. It felt just like old times. We ordered the same things as we did on our first visit—chocolate pastry and cold coffee.

As we sat there, holding hands and gazing into each other's eyes, an idea struck me. A spark of excitement lit up my voice as I said, "I want to play the violin, the same tune you taught me that day."

"Are you sure?"

"Damn, sure. You'll be surprised how quickly I learned."
"Okay, then show me."

At that time, we didn't have a violin, so I went to Rustom Uncle, the owner of Cyrus' Corner, and asked him to lend me the violin from his private collection in the music room. Uncle knew me well—he was fond of me like a daughter because I was a regular customer at Cyrus' Corner. He agreed without hesitation.

I placed the violin under my chin and held the bow steady. Slowly, I started playing the tune that Chirag had taught me. As the music filled the hall, I closed my eyes, letting myself get lost in the melody. The sound seemed to lift me away from the city, and I felt my soul free with the music. My chest tightened, and my throat burned.

Suddenly, I heard clapping. I opened my eyes and saw everyone in the hall standing and applauding. Even Chirag was clapping, joining them in praise.

With tears of happiness and pride, I walked to my table. Chirag looked at me, clearly surprised. He said, "My God, Rishika, you played so well! I didn't know you could learn this tune so quickly."

"You don't know, I practiced every day," I replied, feeling proud.

We spent some time enjoying our pastries and cold coffee. On our way back from Cyrus's Corner, Chirag suddenly said, "I need to go to the gym."

I was confused. "For a workout?"

"No," he said, "I need to go to close my gym account and clear out my locker, take all my things."

"Okay, let's go," I said.

We walked through the streets to the gym. Outside, Chirag stopped and told me, "You wait here. I'll be back soon."

"Why can't I come with you? And don't tell me this gym is only for men. Don't say I shouldn't go in just because all the guys here look at me like I'm a piece of cake," I said, irritated.

He hesitated for a moment but then nodded. We entered and made our way to the locker area. Chirag unlocked the locker with his key. I noticed the same black backpack I had seen during my last visit. Chirag carefully took it out, slinging it over his shoulder. He didn't take anything else from the locker, not the gloves, socks, towels, or any of the other men's items I saw inside.

"Aren't you taking those?" I motioned toward the things in the locker. "You said you needed to empty it."

He chuckled, "Those are nothing. I don't need them anymore."

He left the locker door open as we headed toward the reception. Chirag told the beautiful receptionist, "I want to close the account and surrender the locker under the name Chirag Kelkar."

After a few formalities, the receptionist handed him a closure slip. He carelessly shoved it into his jeans pocket, and we left the gym.

We rushed to our flat to grab our bags. Once we had them, we planned to head straight to the railway station and leave the city for our beautiful destination—Kovalam. I shouted in excitement.

"But you forgot something," he said.

"What?" I asked, confused.

"Your phone is at the repair shop."

"Oh, right! We need to go there first."

At the mobile repair shop, the guy was really sweet. He had fixed my phone and handed it back to me just in time. "Madam, you've received several calls from a girl named Sara," he said as he returned the phone.

My heart skipped a beat. Sara? What was going on? Why was she calling me? It had to be something work-related, probably about a coding task or something. Maybe the office needed me to handle some Python job. What on Earth was going on?

CHAPTER XIX

I didn't want to call Sara back. The memories of our last encounter rushed into my mind like a nightmare I couldn't escape. That day, we had a heated argument—her words still burned in my ears.

She accused me of kissing her that night. I stayed over at her place. She brought up vile things about me and Chirag, things that felt like daggers aimed straight at my heart. Sara always had a problem with my relationship with Chirag. But that wasn't all. That same day, I received a one-month notice from the company. Fired. Just like that. Everything fell apart, and Sara's words made it worse.

Those bitter memories were suffocating me. "Oh, shit!" I screamed. It was the same time I was supposed to leave this city with Chirag to start a fresh, happy life together. And just like a storm, she returned. "Oh, shit!" I yelled again, my voice cracking.

Then my phone buzzed, vibrating angrily in my palm. It was Sara. My heart raced as if it wanted to leap out of my chest. I didn't want to talk to her. I couldn't. My fingers clenched the phone so tightly I thought it might break. For a moment, I wanted to fling it, to escape her voice and everything it brought with it.

But I froze.

"What are you doing?" Chirag's voice was loud and sharp. He looked upset as he saw me yelling at Sara.

"I don't want to talk to her!" I snapped back, my voice just as loud.

Chirag's tone softened. "Talk to her, Rishika. If Sara is a problem, face it. Running away will only make it worse." Then his voice turned stern again, and his words hit me like a slap.

Reluctantly, I grabbed my phone, put it on speaker, and answered the call. My heart raced as Sara's voice came through, the voice I had desperately wanted to avoid.

"Hello, Rishika," Sara said.

I hesitated but finally replied in a low voice, "Hello."

"Where have you been since last night? I've been trying to reach you all morning!" Her tone was sharp as if she were accusing me of something.

"My phone wasn't working. I just got it fixed. What's the matter, Sara? Why were you calling me so much?" I asked, trying to sound casual but feeling anything but.

"Rishika, I want to ask you something," she said, her voice calm but full of tension.

"What is it?" I asked nervously.

Sara paused for a moment, enough to make my stomach tighten. Then she dropped the question.

"What were you doing at the abandoned chemical factory outside the city late last night?"

My heart stopped for a moment. I froze and looked at Chirag. His face had turned serious, his eyes filled with concern.

"What... what are you saying?" I asked hesitantly, my voice shaky.

"Don't play games, Rishika. I saw you there. You were about to climb the boundary wall of that factory to escape. I was there too... with the police."

Her words hit me like a slap. Sara had seen everything. My heart raced, and I glanced at Chirag, whose face mirrored my panic.

Sara's revelation spiked the tension between us. But instead of addressing the seriousness of the situation, I decided to mess with her. "A chemical factory with the police? Wow, Sara. Let me guess—you've joined the night police patrol, haven't you? Daddy pulled a few strings for his favorite rich girl?"

My voice dripped with sarcasm. I hadn't forgotten how, last time, she boasted about her influential father and how he didn't want her associating with someone like me. But now? Now she was here, accusing me, and I needed to buy time to think.

"Stop talking nonsense, Rishika!" Sara snapped. "You don't even know the full story. Let me tell you what happened. Yesterday, at the office, some goons barged in and dragged J.K. away in front of everyone. We were stunned! We called the police immediately, but nothing happened for hours.

"By night, J.K.'s younger brother called me, begging for my help to find him. I couldn't ignore it, so I contacted the commissioner—he's like family to me. After that, the police finally got serious. They tracked J.K.'s phone and found its last location—a chemical factory outside the city.

"We rushed there with the police, hoping to find J.K. alive. But what we saw... it was horrifying."

Sara paused, her voice trembling. She took a deep breath before continuing, "We found J.K.'s dead body. Not just his—there were several others too. The whole place was chaos. And then, I saw you!" she said, her voice rising. "I saw you jumping over the factory's boundary wall! For God's sake, Rishika, what were you doing there?"

Her final words echoed, filled with frustration and anger.

I didn't say a word, but my heart was pounding like a drum. My grip on Chirag's hand tightened.

"Do you have anything to do with J.K.'s murder?" Sara's voice grew louder, sharper.

I stayed silent.

"Oh, for God's sake! Rishi, tell me something! Don't keep me in suspense. Last night, when I saw you there, I could've called the police. But I didn't—I wanted to hear it from you first. Now, if you won't talk, maybe it's better if I just tell the police what I saw. Let them deal with you." Her tone cut like a knife.

What did I do? Nothing. I kept my mouth shut.

"Fine!" Sara snapped. "If that's how it is, I'm hanging up."

"Wait!" I blurted out, my voice breaking. "I'll tell you everything... but not over the phone."

"Then how?"

"Let's meet."

"Where?"

"At your home," I replied, hoping she would agree.

Without saying another word, she hung up. My heart pounded as I stared at the phone, wondering if I had made the right decision.

After nearly an hour, I stood in front of Sara's flat. This was the last place I wanted to be. I had promised myself never to return here. But fate had its own plans. In another life, I would have been on a train to Kovalam with Chirag by now.

Taking a deep breath, I pressed the doorbell. The door creaked open, and there she was—Sara. Or at least, it looked like Sara. I swear, something about her felt off. Her eyes held a strange coldness as if I was a stranger she barely recognized. She didn't speak, didn't invite me in. Without a word, she turned and walked away, leaving the door open behind her. It was an unspoken cue for me to enter.

I stepped inside, and Chirag followed closely. I gave him a quick signal to stay in the drawing room. He nodded, understanding, as I walked deeper into the flat, heading toward Sara's room.

Inside, Sara sat at the edge of her bed. Her face was tense, her eyes red and swollen from crying. Anger and sorrow seemed to swirl around her, filling the room with a heavy, suffocating silence.

I hesitated for a moment, then sat down on the opposite side of the bed, facing her. Her gaze burned through me, but I couldn't back away. Slowly, I reached out my hand toward hers and softly asked, "What happened?"

She pulled her hand back quickly, avoiding mine. "Just tell me, Rishi. What happened to you?" she asked, her voice trembling slightly.

"Nothing," I said, shrugging. "Nothing at all."

"Are you in some kind of trouble?"

"No," I muttered under my breath, barely audible. "All the problems are taken care of now."

Her eyes narrowed as she leaned closer. "Have you done something wrong?"

"No," I whispered again, almost to myself. "Except dragging J.K. into my mess. That's something I'll regret forever."

Her expression hardened, and then suddenly, she snapped. "Then what were you doing at the chemical factory late last night?" she yelled, springing off the bed.

The sharpness in her voice startled me. I flinched, almost jumping out of my seat.

"Calm down, Sara," I said softly, trying to soothe her. "I'm right here. No need to shout." I didn't want Chirag to hear us arguing. He had a short temper, and if he got involved, things could spiral out of control.

Sara glared at me for a moment, her gaze piercing. Then, as if trying to compose herself, she turned away. Her chest rose and fell rapidly, her breath coming in short, quick bursts.

"I swear, I'm telling you the truth, but please don't jump to conclusions," I said, my voice trembling. I took a deep breath before continuing, "It's true. J.K. was dragged out of the office by those goons and taken to that old, abandoned chemical factory... because of me."

Sara's eyes widened in shock. Her mouth opened as if to say something, but I quickly cut her off. "But listen to me—his death wasn't my fault! I never wanted him to die. We even went there to save him. But... we failed. And when the police arrived, we panicked. We ran. We didn't know what else to do."

Her eyebrows shot up as she caught onto something. "You said 'we'? Who else was with you?"

"Chirag," I admitted, my voice barely a whisper.

As soon as I said his name, Sara's expression changed. She leaped up from the edge of the bed, her hair falling wildly over her face as she began pacing the room. Her fists clenched, and she punched her leg with each step, muttering under her breath. She looked like she'd lost her mind.

Sara screamed, "Oh, God, Rishika, not again!"

Her reaction startled me. "What happened to you?" I asked, watching her closely.

She gave me a sly grin. "Forget me. Keep going with your story. Tell me why you said you're responsible for the goons dragging J.K. from the office to that place."

I hesitated for a moment but then admitted, "Because I lied to Raj. I told him J.K. gave me all the cash I used to repay Ramesh Reddy's loan."

Sara's confusion was evident. "Raj? Wait, the police told me Raj Reddy, the owner of CredZone, was also killed in that factory shooting!"

"Yes," I said, my voice heavy. "And Raj was Ramesh Reddy's younger brother."

Her eyes narrowed as she tried to piece things together. "But why did you lie to Raj about J.K. giving you the money? You told me you repaid Ramesh's loan with your freelancing work."

I sighed and looked away. "I lied to you, too. I got the money from... someone else."

Sara's expression turned sharp. "From whom?" she demanded, leaning closer.

I stayed silent, avoiding her gaze. My eyes wandered across the room, searching for an escape from her probing.

Sara began pacing slowly, her mind clearly racing. I knew her well. She was sharp, her logical reasoning like a blade cutting through secrets. If I didn't tread carefully, she would uncover everything.

Sara suddenly froze, her eyes locking onto mine. "You mentioned J.K. before, Raj, to protect the real person who gave you the money, didn't you?" she asked, her voice sharp.

I hesitated before replying, "Yes."

Her lips curled into a triumphant smile. "How did that person get the money?" she pressed, sounding like a detective on a case.

"From his sources in Mumbai," I muttered, avoiding her gaze.

Sara leaned closer, her voice rising. "No, sweetheart. That person got the money by robbing CredZone. And he gave you stolen money, didn't he? I'm right, aren't I?"

"Enough!" I shouted, my voice cracking. "Don't ever say that again!"

My outburst startled Sara. For a moment, she just stared at me, her expression shifting from confidence to unease.

"Are you okay?" she asked softly, her tone almost apologetic.

I took a shaky breath. "No, I'm not okay. Every time someone says Chirag robbed that money, I feel like... like I could strangle them for even suggesting it," I said, my voice echoing off the walls.

"Rishi," she said gently, stepping closer. Her hand rested on my shoulder, steadying me. "I'm talking about what happened last

Saturday—the 10th of October. Not the incident from last year."

I couldn't understand what Sara had just said. Her words brought back the faces of those who had haunted my thoughts—Ramesh Reddy, Raj Reddy, SI Vijay. All of them had told me the same thing: the money I got from Chirag to repay my loan was suspicious. And now, all of them were dead. Sara was repeating it again, and I felt my chest tighten with anger and fear.

She looked straight at me and said, "Rishi, tell me— who gave you that cash?"

I snapped back, my voice sharp. "It was Chirag. Chirag gave me the money! What's your problem with that?"

Her reaction startled me. She jumped up and began pacing the room like a caged animal. This time, she nervously bit her nails, completely forgetting how much effort she had put into shaping them perfectly. They looked beautiful, but she didn't seem to care anymore.

I watched her and thought to myself, *She's lost it. Sara has gone mad.*

I couldn't stand watching her pace back and forth in that tiny room. It was unbearable. I knew I had to tell her everything—the secrets I had kept hidden for so long.

Taking a deep breath, I began, "Chirag gave me the money. I used it to repay my loan to Ramesh. But he suspected it was stolen money from CredZone. To clear his doubts, Chirag went to his house and spoke to him. But after Chirag left, Ramesh's younger brother, Raj, killed him."

SI Vijay and Raj wanted to frame us for the robbery and Ramesh's murder. They kidnapped me, demanding to know who gave me the money. I didn't want to betray Chirag, so I gave them another name—J.K. That was my mistake.

When Chirag and I realized the danger, we decided to confront them. Last night, we went to that abandoned factory. Raj, Vijay, and their men were waiting to kill us. They fired at us, but Chirag saved me. He fought them off and killed them all.

Then we heard the sirens. The police were closing in. We panicked and ran – we couldn't afford to get tangled up with the law.

"That's when you saw me. I had to come here after that. Otherwise, Chirag and I had a plan. We were going to catch a train and leave this wretched city for good."

CHAPTER XX

After saying all that, I glanced at Sara. She had been silently listening to me, her eyes occasionally widening at the things I said. But then, she started laughing. It wasn't a nervous chuckle—it was full-blown laughter as if I'd just told her the funniest joke. She laughed for a good twenty seconds, acting like everything I had said was perfectly normal.

Finally, she managed to catch her breath and said, "Seriously, Rishika? You and Chirag? Oh, my God."

Her laughter made me furious. Why was she laughing at the mention of Chirag's name? I clenched my fists, wishing I could shut her up forever.

"In that case, Chirag is a killer, isn't he?" she said, her tone suddenly serious.

"No!" I screamed so loud that my throat hurt. "Chirag didn't kill them—he defended himself! That's not the same as murder. And if you ever say that again, I swear I'll strangle you with my bare hands!"

Sara froze her face, a mix of shock and anger. Maybe I should have done it already—taught her a lesson. But instead, she quietly picked up her phone from the table.

"Rishika, you need Dr. Neelam," she said flatly while dialing a number.

Her words made my blood boil.

"Why?" I asked through gritted teeth.

"Because you've lost your mind, obsessing over Chirag like this," she replied, her disgust clear in her eyes.

"Yes, I've gone crazy for Chirag. Do you have a problem with that? Is it wrong for a girl to fall in love with a guy?" I asked.

"No problem, Rishi, with a girl falling in love with a guy, but if you fall in love with Chirag—now that's a problem. A big problem," Sara said, still distracted by her phone.

"What's the problem?" I asked, confused.

"Why? You don't know? Face the reality, Rishi," she replied, looking at me with fake concern.

"What's with this 'face the reality' talk? Am I dreaming or what?" I asked, bewildered.

Sara smirked. "Yes, you're dreaming about Chirag. But guess what? Chirag isn't here."

"What the hell are you saying? Chirag is right here!" I said, surprised.

"Where? I don't see him," she laughed at me.

Just then, I smelled it—the familiar scent of a Cuban cigar, the one I loved. I turned around. There he was—Chirag, surrounded by a thick cloud of cigar smoke, looking like something out of a dream.

Sara screamed, "Rishika, what are you doing?"

Chirag smiled at me and said, "Don't worry, Rishika. I'm here now. I'll show this girl just how real I am. Damn real."

Sara was sitting on the floor, both furious and frightened. When I saw her like that, I felt a strange satisfaction. She kept repeating, "Stop doing this."

Chirag walked in and sat down in front of her, locking eyes with her. He took a deep drag of his cigar and blew the smoke right in her face. Sara coughed, clearly disgusted. Chirag grabbed her hand, but she pushed him away and ran out of the room. She hid in the washroom in the corridor.

Chirag laughed. "Did you see her face? She turned pale when she saw me."

I felt pleased, too, but then a thought hit me. Panic rose in my chest. I yelled, "Chirag, she took her phone with her into the washroom! She might be calling someone—maybe the police! She could tell them about us, about what happened last night—about how we were there, and you killed everyone. Our whole plan will be ruined."

"No, Rishika, don't worry," Chirag said, rushing toward the corridor. "She won't call anyone."

He hurried to the washroom door and started knocking.

"Sara!" I shouted, banging on the door.

"Sara!" Chirag echoed, knocking louder.

We tried calling her many times, but there was no answer. With each passing second, my tension grew. I shouted again, "Sara!" Then, it hit me. I had told Chirag to stay quiet, so I quickly stopped him from making any noise. I pressed my ear against the washroom door, and that's when I heard Sara's voice. She was talking to someone.

A wave of fear rushed through me. I whispered to Chirag, "Chirag, she's talking to someone on the phone. She must have called the police. She knows about us. We can't let the police ruin our plan to go to Kovalam."

I saw Chirag's brown eyes darken with anger, turning red with rage. He pulled me away from the door and stepped back. Without warning, he slammed his shoulder against the door. One, two, three – and then, with a loud crash, the door broke open.

Inside, I saw Sara. Her face drained of color when she saw us. She screamed in terror, then sank to the floor, covering her ears and eyes with her hands, shaking with fear.

"You bitch! Calling the police and telling them about us. You wanted us behind bars!" I shouted, kneeling down in front of her.

Her voice trembled, "No, I wasn't talking to the police."

"You're lying!" I snapped.

"No, I'm not lying. Please, don't do this. Let me go," she begged, her eyes wide with fear.

I took a deep breath, trying to stay calm. "I'll let you go, but only if you apologize for calling Chirag a killer." I didn't want to hurt Sara—she used to be my friend. I would let her leave, but she had to say sorry to Chirag first.

But then something unexpected happened. As I stood there, lost in thought, Sara suddenly shoved me hard. I was already on my knees, so I lost my balance. My head slammed into the bathtub, and I felt my skin tear open. Blood started to drip down. At that moment, I saw Sara running away.

But she didn't get far. Chirag grabbed her leg, and she stumbled, her body crashing into the bathtub. The water in the tub splashed onto the floor as she sank into it.

Chirag rushed over and helped me to my feet. He gently pushed my hair aside to check the cut on my head. Pain shot through me, and I could see the fury in his eyes as he clenched his teeth.

I turned back to Sara. Her head was bleeding, too, but there was something different about her. It was as if the injury had pushed her over the edge. She screamed at me, "Rishika, you bitch! You're totally mad. Go to hell with your criminal lover, Chirag!"

Sara's harsh words set Chirag off. In a flash, he lunged at her and grabbed her neck with both hands. His face was twisted with anger. He squeezed tighter, and Sara's body fought against his grip. Her nails dug into his skin as her legs flailed in the water. I was terrified. I had wanted Sara to learn a lesson for her teasing and her rude behavior toward Chirag, but I never imagined I'd see her die right in front of me, with Chirag's hands around her neck.

I screamed, desperately trying to pull Chirag away. "Chirag, what are you doing? Stop! She's learned her lesson!"

But he wouldn't listen. His grip on her neck remained firm as he spoke like a man gone mad. "Now tell me I'm a criminal. Tell me I'm a killer. Yes, I'm the killer. I killed Ramesh and all his allies. I even robbed the money from CredZone. What will you do? Go ahead, tell the police, bitch."

I froze, shocked by his words. Had he killed Ramesh Reddy and robbed CredZone?

But saving Sara from him was more important right now. I tried again to pull his hands off, but he shoved me away. In the struggle, I grabbed the strap of his backpack, and it fell to the floor. It was the same bag he had taken from his gym locker earlier.

I fell to my knees, crying. "Please, Chirag, don't do this. Don't kill Sara. Please, don't."

Tears blurred my vision as I slapped his hands, but it was no use. Sara's legs were still, floating in the water, her body lifeless. Her eyes were wide open, staring at the ceiling. Chirag, sweating and breathing heavily, finally released his grip. Her body sank completely into the water.

She was gone.

I rushed to her, holding her face in my hands. My heart broke as I screamed, "You monster! You killed my friend." I sobbed uncontrollably as I closed Sara's eyes, my hands trembling.

CHAPTER XXI

When I came back to my senses, I found myself on a deserted dirt road. The cold wind stung my skin, and the silence of the night felt heavy. I didn't know where I was. All I knew was that Chirag had dragged me away, gripping my wrists tightly from Sara's flat. My mind was a blur, shattered by what I had just witnessed.

I didn't want to remember, but Sara's lifeless body refused to leave my thoughts. Her wide-open eyes stared at me, empty and haunting. Tears welled up again, and my chest burned with grief and anger.

"You killed her!" I screamed at Chirag, my voice cracking. "You killed my best friend, Sara! You monster!"

Chirag's face turned pale, startled by my outburst. He tried to speak, his tone unnervingly calm. "Look, I understand that—"

"No, you don't!" I cut him off, shaking with fury. "You'll never understand! Love, friendship, loyalty—these are feelings you'll never have! You're heartless, Chirag! A stone-hearted monster!"

I collapsed to my knees, covering my face with trembling hands. Memories of Sara began flashing in my mind, vivid and raw. Her laughter, her warm hugs, her silly jokes—everything that made her my best friend played like a reel, one moment after another.

The weight of her absence crushed me. How could she be gone? How could someone so full of life now only exist in my memories?

And it was all because of Chirag.

Chirag tapped my shoulder, but I shoved him away. He frowned, his voice firm but low, "Rishika, staying here isn't safe. Look, I know we missed the train to Kovalam, but we should head to the station. We might find another one."

His words lit a fire inside me. I shot him a sharp glare, my head high, my eyes burning with fury. Chirag took a cautious step back, his hands slightly raised as if trying to calm a wild animal.

I spat the words at him like venom, "You still think I'd go anywhere with you? You—a killer, a thief, and God knows what else I haven't discovered yet."

He stared at me, his face a mix of confusion and frustration. "What are you saying, Rishika? Yes, I killed those men at the factory last night, but they were a threat to us! I did it for us!"

Despite the sharp ache in my chest, I laughed—a bitter, hollow sound. "Oh, my savior, is that what you think you are?" I paused, my voice dripping with sarcasm, before continuing, "I'm not talking about the factory, Chirag. I'm talking about the robbery at CredZone. About Ramesh Reddy. About Sara."

My throat tightened with the weight of my own words. I couldn't say more. My pain choked me like a noose.

Chirag didn't respond. He just turned his face away, his gaze fixed on the faint glow of a distant streetlamp. The deserted road stretched around us, silent and suffocating in the dead of night.

Chirag said, "Rishika, I made a mistake. I didn't mean to hurt Sara. But when she said something wrong about us, I lost control. In my anger, I said I robbed CredZone and killed Ramesh. But I swear, I didn't do it."

His words hit me like a thunderclap. My blood boiled. Without thinking, I stood up, stormed over to him, and started hitting him.

"You liar! You're a cheater, a big liar!" I shouted, my voice shaking with rage.

"Rishika, stop! Listen to me! You're misunderstanding everything!" Chirag said, brushing his messy hair off his face, his voice desperate.

"Listen to you? My foot!" I snapped. In one swift move, I snatched his backpack off his shoulder. Ignoring his protests, I unzipped it and dumped everything out onto the dusty road.

What fell out made my heart sink: a heap of cash bundles tied with a thin white strip, a gun, and an old Nokia mobile phone.

I pointed at the cash, my hands trembling. "This! This is the truth you've been hiding!" I yelled, my voice breaking. "These bundles are tied with the same white strip as Raj told me. They're proof this money came from there! And it was in your bag—the same bag I found in your gym locker! Everything points to you, Chirag. You're the one who robbed CredZone. You're the one who killed Ramesh!"

My chest felt heavy with betrayal as tears blurred my vision. I had trusted him, defended him against everyone who doubted him. And now, here he stood, exposed for what he really was—the man I loved had become my worst nightmare.

Chirag froze in shock, his voice trembling as he whispered, "How do you know this backpack has cash from CredZone?"

I stared at him, my voice steady but cold. "When you were busy killing Sara, and I tried to stop you, your backpack strap tore in the chaos. The bag fell, and the cash bundles spilled out. It was impossible to miss."

He stood silently, like a statue, his face pale. I walked up to him and slapped him over and over, snapping my fingers near his face. "You liar, you cheat!" I shouted. "You played with my feelings. You didn't love me. You just used me—my body, my soul!"

"Stop it, Rishika!" Chirag suddenly yelled, his voice cracking. Tears welled up in his eyes, and I froze mid-slap. He grabbed my hand, holding it tightly, and said, "Don't say I used you. Don't say I didn't love you."

He looked deep into my eyes, his brown eyes filled with a raw emotion that once made me fall for him. "I love you," he said, his voice barely above a whisper. "From the moment I first saw you, I loved you. Everything I did, no matter how horrible, I did it for you."

I felt a chill run down my spine as he continued, his voice heavy with guilt. "I stole the money from CredZone because you needed it to pay Ramesh. If you didn't, he might've hurt you. I killed him because he was about to call the police. After I beat him, I forced him to make that apology video for you. I know I lied to you, but I did it all to protect you."

He paused, his words cutting deeper than I expected. "Yes, I'm a thief. I'm a killer. And there's more. My past is filled with crimes I never told you about."

His confession hung in the air, and the man I thought I loved suddenly felt like a stranger.

I froze as his words sank in. The truth he revealed left me speechless. I didn't want to say anything, yet curiosity gripped me when he confessed, "I have a criminal past."

He looked straight at me, his voice steady but haunting. "Yes, I was a criminal. I've committed many crimes in my life. I'm from Bengal, and my real name is Saumitra Sen. My name is used in every police station in Bengal and even in neighboring states.

Police from several states are hunting me. They've kept my phone under surveillance. Look at that." He pointed to the old Nokia mobile phone lying abandoned on the road, which had fallen from his backpack.

I followed his gaze, noticing the worn-out device. "That phone," he continued, "is my only connection to the police. If I switch it on, they'll track me down in minutes. Without it, they don't know my whereabouts. To them, I'm just a ghost."

A chill ran down my spine. My heart pounded louder with every word he spoke, but he chuckled softly, his eyes locking with mine. I turned my face away, trying to process it all, but his voice followed me.

"Rishika," he said, his tone gentler now, "I've done so many wrong things that I became exhausted with the life I was leading. I escaped it all and came to Bengaluru to start fresh. Once, I dreamed of being a writer, and I thought I could make that dream real here. My past gave me plenty of stories—dark, thrilling ones. So, I rented a flat and tried to live quietly.

"Then I met you. You, my beautiful neighbor, changed everything. For the first time, I dreamed of something pure—of a peaceful life with you in a small house near a lake, surrounded by nature. But that dream... my 'Kovalam' plan... I've ruined it myself." His voice cracked as he finished, and he let out a heavy sigh.

He stepped closer, but I instinctively turned away again. "I know," he said, "you can't even look at me after learning who I truly am. But, Rishika, I love you. I always will, until my last breath wherever I lived, wherever I go."

Then he left.

CHAPTER XXII

Chirag's words still echoed in my mind, heavy and impossible to ignore. Fear and disbelief swirled inside me, mixing with something I couldn't quite place. Was it pity? Or something darker?

I sat alone on the balcony of my flat, surrounded by the distant hum of Bengaluru's chaos. My eyes rested on the areca palm planted in a small pot, the one Chirag had planted for me. I reached out and brushed the leaves gently, my mind drowning in thoughts. How did it all come to this? I never imagined things would end this way. It was over. Everything was over.

The faint smell of Cuban cigar smoke broke through my thoughts. Startled, I looked up. My heart stopped. There he was—on the balcony right next to mine, standing exactly where I had first seen him, smiling with his piercing brown eyes, a cigar between his fingers. Fear gripped me like ice.

I knew why he was here. He must have known. Why would a murderer spare the girl who told the police about him? I wanted to run, but my legs wouldn't move. Before I could even try, his voice cut through the tension like a knife.

"Stop, Rishika!"

I froze. Slowly, I turned back to face him. He took a long drag from his cigar, then exhaled the smoke in my direction. His voice was calm, but it carried a razor-sharp edge.

"Don't go anywhere," he said, his eyes locked onto mine. "I don't have much time."

My legs were trembling, but I gathered all my courage and spoke, "The police are after you."

"I know," he replied, his lips curling into a calm smile. "And it's all because of you."

Yes, I had tipped off the police after Chirag revealed his identity to me late last night. From a telephone booth, I made the call, careful to hide my own identity. I told them everything—that Chirag was planning to flee the city. What choice did I have? He had betrayed me, taken away my only friend, Sara, and trapped me in his web of lies and crime. All because of his so-called "favor" of giving me money.

But why was he here? I thought he'd already left the city, that he'd be at the railway station, bus stand, or maybe the airport. Why come here?

"Sorry... I..." My words faltered, my mind a chaotic mess. He just stood there, smiling, his sharp gaze locked on mine.

After a shaky breath, I forced out the question: "If you know the police are after you, why did you come here?"

"Where else would I go?" he said, his voice cold and steady. "Where else would I go... for this task?"

Task? What task? The realization hit me like a bolt of lightning. He was here to kill me.

My heart raced, thundering in my chest, as a cold sweat ran down my back. Everything suddenly made sense.

He slid his right hand into the pocket of his blue denim jacket. My heart pounded—I was sure he had a 9mm pistol in there. He was going to kill me. I squeezed my eyes shut, waiting for the end. So, this was it. My life would end at the hands of the man who was once my love, my world, my biggest support.

But then... nothing happened.

When he pulled his hand out, it wasn't a gun. Instead, it was an old Nokia phone—the same one I'd noticed for the first time last night. He powered it on, and the familiar start-up tune played. The sound took me back to my childhood, to the days when I used to switch my dad's phone on and off just to hear that tone.

He placed the phone on the edge of the balcony railing, the orange glow of his cigar lighting up his face. "I made it easy for them," he said, his voice calm, almost detached. "The police will find me soon. They'll track this phone." He took another drag, letting the smoke curl around him like a ghost.

I remembered his words from the night before. He had told me how his number was already on the police's radar, linked to a trail of crimes. "The moment I turn it on, they'll come for me," he'd explained.

Even now, I couldn't understand him. I rubbed my temples, confusion and fear swirling in my mind. "Why are you doing this?" I finally asked, my voice shaky.

He didn't answer immediately. He just looked out at the dark skyline, his face unreadable. Then, in that deep voice I once loved so much, he said, "Do me a favor."

"A favor?" I asked, unsure where this was going. "What kind of favor?"

"Play the violin, the tune which I taught you," he said simply, his tone soft but commanding.

"Violin?" I stammered, caught completely off guard.

"Yes," he said, taking another puff. "Play for me the tune. One last time... before they come."

His eyes looked far away, lost in thoughts I couldn't reach.

I couldn't figure him out. Was he waiting for me to play music before killing me? Gathering my courage, I asked, "Aren't you going to kill me?"

He laughed softly. "Kill you? How could I do that? You're my love. And maybe you don't remember, but I saved your life once, right here. Now stop wasting time and play."

His words confused me, but I did as he said. I went inside, picked up my violin, and returned to the balcony. Standing in front of him, I placed the violin under my chin, gripped the bow, and began to play.

As the gentle notes filled the night air, the past few days replayed in my mind like a movie. Tears started streaming down my cheeks, and I didn't know why. Who was he to me? A murderer. That's all he was. But still, the emotions were too much for me to handle.

I kept my eyes closed, but I knew he hadn't left. The faint smell of his cigar lingered in the cool air. He stayed quiet, listening to every note.

I knew the police were on their way. Any moment now, they'd burst in. But he didn't try to escape. He just stood there, still as a statue, listening to the music.

Who was this man? What kind of person listens to music while waiting to get caught?

My hands slowed, the music fading into silence. Sirens wailed in the distance, growing louder with each passing second. My heart pounded like a drum. Could I help him hide? Should I? He was a murderer.

"Don't stop!" His voice cut through my panic. It made me shiver. "Keep playing!"

I obeyed, my fingers shaking as they touched the violin strings. The melody was shaky, but I kept going. Two police cars screeched to a stop far below. I heard heavy boots pounding up the stairs. They were coming closer. Too close.

Why wasn't he running? Why wasn't he trying to escape?

I glanced at him. He was smiling—calm, even amused. The cigar in his hand was almost gone, and he tossed it aside carelessly. Then, in one shocking moment, he stepped onto the edge of the balcony.

I froze; my breath caught in my throat.

And then he jumped.

From the ninth floor.

My scream stuck in my chest, and before I could react, he grabbed my hand. His grip was firm, unyielding.

The next thing I knew, we were falling.

Together.

Hand in hand.

The wind whipped past us, but he looked at me and smiled. I couldn't help but smile back despite the terror rushing through me.

"Thank you, Chirag," I whispered, my voice barely audible over the wind. "What a perfect ending. I couldn't live without you."

Thud.

Epilogue

ACP stepped into the police commissioner's office and saluted before handing over a red file. The commissioner, a man in his late fifties nearing retirement next month, took the file with a tired sigh.

"I hope this is the final closure report," he said, his voice heavy with expectation.

"Yes, sir," ACP responded, standing straight.

"Good. Now tell me, what did you uncover?" the commissioner asked, leaning forward.

ACP began, his tone serious. "Sir, as you know, between the 10th and 16th of October, we faced four major crimes that rocked the city. First, the robbery at CredZone. Second, the murder of senior banker Ramesh Reddy. Third, the violent shootout and mass killing at the chemical factory on the city outskirts. And lastly, the murder of Sara Rao, daughter of the renowned criminal lawyer Virendra Rao." He paused for a moment, letting the weight of his words sink in. "Sir, all these crimes were committed by one person—Rishika Kapoor, resident of flat number A 904, Blue Sky Apartments. She orchestrated everything."

The commissioner raised his eyebrows. "And when you went to arrest her, she committed suicide by jumping off the ninth floor?"

"Yes, Sir," ACP confirmed. "But her suicide was... unusual. When we broke into her flat, we found her standing on the balcony. She didn't react to our presence, didn't even glance our way. Her eyes were fixed on the balcony next door like she was staring at someone—or something. Then, suddenly, her body jerked as if an invisible force struck her. She jumped right after that. It didn't seem like she was afraid of being caught. It felt like something else was at play."

The commissioner adjusted his glasses and leaned closer to the photographs in the file. One photo made him freeze. It showed a young woman—Rishika Kapoor—lying lifeless on the ground, her body twisted as though she had fallen from a height. Blood pooled beneath her head, and her eyes, wide open, seemed distant yet strangely captivating. For a moment, he couldn't tear his gaze away.

He broke the silence. "So, you're saying this young, 23-year-old beautiful tech professional, Rishika Kapoor, is behind all these crimes?"

"Yes, sir," the ACP replied firmly.

The commissioner frowned. "Do you have solid evidence to prove it?"

"Yes, Sir," the ACP said, his voice calm but serious. "Let me explain everything step by step. Let's start with the first case—the robbery at CredZone. Rishika attacked the guards, broke the lock, took the cash, and escaped with a black backpack."

He paused, letting the weight of his words sink in.

"Here's something interesting," he continued. "Her office cab driver gave a statement. He said that for a week before the robbery, Rishika would ask him to stop near the crime spot. Normally, her stop is two kilometers away."

The officer sitting across the table narrowed his eyes. "Are you saying she planned this robbery a week in advance?"

The ACP nodded. "It certainly looks that way."

The commissioner raised an eyebrow. "Does the CCTV footage support this? Was her face visible?"

"No, Sir. The footage shows the robber wearing a black hoodie, hiding their face. But the black backpack used in the robbery was found in Rishika's flat. Inside it, we recovered ₹ 20 lakhs tied with CredZone-labeled strips."

The commissioner leaned back, skeptical. "What do you mean by 'CredZone-labeled'?"

The ACP clarified, "CredZone uses a unique white paper strip to bundle cash. Their brand name is printed on it in very tiny letters, almost invisible to the naked eye."

The commissioner paused, thinking. "Hmm. But what if someone planted the backpack in her flat to frame her?"

ACP replied, "No, sir, it's not like that. After the robbery, Rishika hid the backpack in a gym locker at Garden City Fitness Gym. We checked the gym's CCTV footage and uncovered the truth."

The commissioner leaned forward, his voice sharp. "How did you link her to this gym?"

ACP explained, "We found a gym account closure receipt in her jeans pocket—on her dead body."

The commissioner pulled out a paper from the file and read it aloud. "This receipt says the account belonged to someone named Chirag Kelkar. Who is this Chirag Kelkar? Wait a minute... I've heard this name before, but I can't place it."

ACP nodded. "Sir, I'll explain everything about Chirag Kelkar later. Right now, let's focus on Rishika Kapoor."

The commissioner tapped the file, his tone growing stern. "Fine, Chirag can wait. All the evidence points to Rishika robbing CredZone. What about her next crime?"

ACP's face darkened. "The next crime was murder. Rishika killed Ramesh Reddy in his own home."

The commissioner narrowed his eyes. "CCTV footage showed someone in a black hoodie entering Ramesh's house. Are you saying that was Rishika?"

ACP nodded firmly. "Yes, Sir. That hooded figure was Rishika—the killer."

The commissioner's voice dropped to a cold whisper. "What's your proof?"

ACP opened another file. "Ramesh was killed with a 9mm gun. We found that same gun inside the backpack in Rishika's flat. Forensics confirmed her fingerprints were all over it. It's the exact gun used in the murder."

The commissioner's brow furrowed as he processed the information. "But why would Rishika kill Ramesh? What was her motive?"

The ACP said, "Ramesh might have known that Rishika robbed CredZone. Maybe he threatened or blackmailed her. We checked Ramesh's phone records, and he called Rishika many times after getting money from her. That's not all. We found a video on Rishika's phone. In the video, Ramesh was there, apologizing to her. He looked like someone had beaten him badly. And then, we saw something shocking. When our technician zoomed in on the footage, we noticed Rishika's reflection in a mirror. She was standing right in front of Ramesh before he was shot. That's when she killed him."

The commissioner leaned forward. "After Ramesh's murder, you told me you suspected Rishika. You sent Sub-Inspector Vijay to take her statement, didn't you?"

"Yes, Sir," the ACP replied. "But I had no idea Vijay was working with Ramesh's younger brother, Raj. After getting Rishika's statement, Vijay reported everything to Raj. They both kidnapped Rishika and took her to an abandoned chemical factory. They wanted to know the truth. They didn't have proof against her but suspected she wasn't working alone."

The commissioner nodded slowly. "Go on."

"At the factory," the ACP continued, "Rishika played a trick. She told Vijay and Raj that her colleague, J.K., was involved. She said J.K. had given her the money."

The commissioner raised an eyebrow. "So, she lied to save herself. Makes sense."

The ACP shook his head. "No, sir. She wasn't trying to save herself. She was protecting someone else."

The commissioner frowned. "Who?"

"Chirag," the ACP said.

The commissioner rubbed his temples. "Chirag... Why does that name sound familiar? Who is he?"

The ACP's expression darkened. "Just wait, sir. I'll explain everything about Chirag soon."

The commissioner leaned forward and asked, "What happened when Rishika mentioned J.K. to them? Did they let her go?"

The ACP shook his head slowly. "Yes, Sir. They took her back to her flat, but Raj wasn't done. He left one of his men to watch her every move."

The commissioner raised an eyebrow. "Hmm."

The ACP continued, "The next day, Vijay took J.K. away from Zenith Networks. They tortured him, trying to get the truth out of him."

"Poor man," the commissioner said with a sigh. "And what did J.K. say? That he didn't know anything about the money? Looks like Rishika framed an innocent man."

The ACP nodded slowly, his expression grim. "When Raj couldn't get any information about the money from J.K.," he began, pausing for effect, "his men brought Rishika back into the factory. But this time, Rishika was ready. Raj and his men had no idea she was hiding a gun."

"And she killed all of them? Raj, Vijay, the goons—everyone? Hard to believe," the commissioner said, his voice laced with disbelief.

"You'll believe it once you know her background," the ACP replied. "Rishika's family is from a military background. Her father was a Major in the Indian Army. She's been trained in advanced martial arts and even won a state-level shooting championship during her college days. That night, she killed them all. But she couldn't save J.K."

The commissioner looked grim. "Forensic reports, CCTV footage, ballistic evidence—all of them pointed to her?"

"Yes, sir," the ACP confirmed. "Everything. And there's more. We have an eyewitness to the massacre."

"An eyewitness?" the commissioner asked, surprised. "You mean Vijay? The corrupt sub-inspector?"

"That's correct, Sir," the ACP said. "Vijay wasn't dead at the scene. He was critically injured and taken to the hospital. Before he died, he gave a full statement. He confirmed everything."

The commissioner leaned forward, his eyes narrowing. "Now, let's get to the last crime committed by Rishika," he said, his voice low but firm.

The ACP straightened up, a somber look on his face. "Rishika killed her best friend and biggest supporter, Sara. She strangled her. Forensics found Rishika's fingerprints on Sara's neck."

The commissioner frowned deeply. "What was the motive for the murder?"

"Anger," the ACP replied.

"Are you saying Rishika was angry with Sara?"

"Yes, sir," the ACP confirmed.

The commissioner's voice grew sharper. "Why? What made her angry?"

"It was because of Chirag," the ACP explained. "Rishika believed Sara insulted Chirag. She thought Sara had called him a thief, a liar, and a cheater."

The commissioner slammed his hand on the desk, and frustration was evident. "Enough! Who is this Chirag? Without understanding him, it's impossible to understand Rishika."

The ACP nodded gravely. "You're right, Sir. Chirag Kelkar is the key to Rishika's story. But before I explain Chirag, I must mention someone else—Dr. Neelam."

The commissioner raised an eyebrow. "Dr. Neelam? The renowned psychiatrist?"

"Yes, sir," the ACP confirmed.

"What's her connection to Rishika?"

The ACP replied, "Rishika was her patient. Sara had taken her to Dr. Neelam because her mental health was deteriorating."

"What was wrong with her?" the commissioner asked.

"She suffered from PTSD—Post-Traumatic Stress Disorder," the ACP said.

"How long had she been struggling with this?"

"Since her parents' death during the Covid-19 pandemic. But things got worse after Chirag's death," the ACP revealed.

The commissioner froze for a moment. "Chirag is dead?"

"Yes, sir," the ACP confirmed.

"When did he die?"

"Six months ago," the ACP said. He took a deep breath before continuing. "I'll tell you the whole story about Chirag. You might recall that six months ago, the STF tracked down Saumitra Sen—a notorious criminal from Bengal and nearby states—when his phone was switched on..."

The commissioner said, "Yes, I remember. How can I forget? But when the STF went there to nab him, he committed suicide by jumping from the ninth floor. Wait, the same thing happened with Rishika this time."

"Absolutely, Sir," ACP said.

"Is there any connection between Rishika and Saumitra?" the commissioner asked.

"Both were neighbors. Their flats were adjacent. Their balconies were adjacent, just five feet apart. But..." ACP said.

"But?" the commissioner asked.

ACP said, "Saumitra was living with a fake identity. He was living in the name of Chirag Kelkar."

The commissioner said, "Now I remember, I heard this name in the case of Saumitra Sen. So, Saumitra, aka Chirag, was dead six months ago. Why is he relevant to Rishika's case?"

ACP said, "They both loved each other. For Rishika, Chirag was everything to her. She was even planning to marry him and live with him somewhere in Kerala."

"Then?"

"One day, she came to know Chirag's reality, and she informed the police about him. Later, as we know, STF got his location by his cell phone. Chirag committed suicide in front of Rishika when STF reached the location," ACP said.

"What happened to Rishika?"

"She went into deep mental shock. Her PTSD increased to the next level. She experienced hallucinations and delusions about Chirag," ACP said.

"Means?"

"This means that since Chirag was dead, Rishika was alive. She could see him, she could touch him, she could even intimate with him, but only in her mind," ACP said.

The commissioner said, "Oh, my God."

"When Rishika took her treatment seriously, she would be cured a bit. But during the past month, she was not taking the treatment seriously and thought that she was good. She didn't take the advice of her best friend Sara, who brought her to Dr Neelam. She didn't talk to Dr Neelam properly about the medication," ACP said.

Suddenly, the ACP's phone buzzed. He glanced at the screen and said, "Sir, I've called Dr. Neelam here to help us understand Rishika's case. She's at the door."

The commissioner nodded and asked the ACP to bring Dr. Neelam into his office.

Dr Neelam entered the room. She was in her late fifties, a thin woman with a sad expression. Dressed in an elegant white saree, she looked calm and composed. After exchanging greetings with the commissioner, she began speaking in a gentle voice.

"Sara was like a daughter to me," she said. "She brought Rishika to me after Chirag's death. Patients like her need support and love. Rishika had no one except Sara, who became her family. During our sessions, Rishika opened up about Chirag. After his death, she started feeling his presence around her. She couldn't separate reality from delusion. She believed the past was still happening."

"With medication and Sara's support, she began to heal. But about a month ago, she stopped coming to the clinic. She thought she didn't need help anymore. Whenever Sara or I reminded her about her medication or therapy, she became violent."

The commissioner frowned. "In that case, Dr. Neelam, why didn't you act forcefully?"

Dr Neelam removed her glasses and wiped them with a tissue. Her voice grew quieter. "Patients like Rishika can't be forced. They aren't criminals."

"But she *has* become one—a dangerous one," the commissioner said firmly.

Dr Neelam sighed. "None of us expected it to turn out like this."

The commissioner leaned forward, his tone sharp. "How did it start, Dr Neelam? What do you think triggered it? Especially the events of last week?"

Dr Neelam hesitated for a moment before speaking, her voice calm but serious. "I remember it clearly," she began. "It was the afternoon of October 9th when Sara called me. She sounded worried. Sara told me that Rishika had been talking about Chirag. But the strange part was that Rishika spoke as if she had seen him the previous night. The problem was Chirag had died a few months ago."

Dr Neelam paused, her gaze fixed on the commissioner, then continued, "It was obvious that her delusions about Chirag had resurfaced. Sara was really concerned and asked me to arrange a session with Rishika. I knew Rishika wouldn't come if I asked her to attend the session. I told Sara I would try inviting Rishika to my marriage anniversary party that evening. I sent her an invitation, but she didn't show up."

The commissioner leaned forward. "What happened next?" he asked.

"I messaged her the following morning," Dr Neelam replied. "I suggested meeting at a restaurant near her apartment—Cyrus' Corner. She agreed and messaged back, confirming the time."

The commissioner's voice sharpened. "And when you met her, what did you say?"

Dr Neelam began, "Our meeting didn't happen as planned. I got to the restaurant late. When I arrived, I saw Rishika playing the violin for the crowd. She played beautifully. I remembered her mentioning in one of our sessions that Chirag had taught her how to play. The people there were cheering for her performance, but her behavior seemed strange. She was talking to an empty chair. A waiter told me she had ordered double as if expecting someone else, but she was alone. While some people thought she was intoxicated, I realized there was more to it. I decided to approach her."

"And then what happened?" the commissioner asked, leaning forward.

Dr Neelam continued, "Before I could reach her, Ramesh Reddy appeared. I hadn't noticed him earlier because the place was so crowded. He stormed over to Rishika and started yelling, demanding she return his money. Rishika looked humiliated and ran out of the restaurant. I followed her, calling out her name, but she didn't respond. Seeing how upset she was, I decided to give her some space and let her be."

The ACP interjected, "Sir, that was the same night the robbery happened at CredZone."

The commissioner turned to Dr Neelam and asked, "What happened after the restaurant incident? Did you speak to Rishika again?"

Dr Neelam nodded. "Yes, I spoke to her the following Sunday morning, on October 11th. I was worried about her. But when we talked, it felt like she wasn't interested. She had completely forgotten that we had planned to meet at the restaurant. I could sense she was in a hurry. She told me she was going for a picnic.

Before I could ask more, she ended the call abruptly. Later, I learned from Sara that Rishika had gone to Nandi Hills. But she wasn't alone—she went with 'Chirag.'"

The commissioner's eyes narrowed. "So, physically, she was alone on her trip to Nandi Hills, but in her mind, she was with Chirag."

"Exactly," Dr Neelam confirmed.

The ACP added, "Sir, we also have a statement from the cab driver who dropped Rishika home late that Sunday night after her trip to Nandi Hills. He said her behavior in the back seat was odd, almost disturbing. It seemed like she was talking to someone who wasn't there. The driver admitted he was frightened by how she acted—it felt like she wasn't alone."

The commissioner leaned forward and asked, "What happened next?"

Dr Neelam took a deep breath and began, "Sara used to share every little detail about Rishika with me. On Monday, 12th October, while they were at the office, Rishika was watching news about a robbery. Sara, in her usual playful tone, joked that Chirag might have been involved. She was just teasing—Sara knew a lot about Chirag but wasn't serious. However, Rishika didn't take it well. She didn't say a word, but her face showed she was furious with Sara.

"By evening, Sara apologized, and things seemed fine for the moment. As they were leaving the office, Sara asked Rishika to show pictures from her trip to Nandi Hills the day before. But when Rishika couldn't find a single photo of Chirag from the trip on her phone, she grew visibly restless and nervous. It was obvious something was wrong. Then, Sara made another joke, saying, 'Maybe Chirag is a ghost!'

"That was the last straw for Rishika. She lost her temper and snapped at Sara. She angrily pulled up an older photo of her with Chirag on her phone, from when he was still alive, and showed it to her. Sara was deeply hurt by Rishika's outburst. She reminded Rishika that she had been skipping therapy sessions with me, but Rishika completely ignored her words."

The ACP narrowed his eyes and asked, "Dr. Neelam, don't you think Sara's teasing remarks about Chirag might have provoked Rishika? Could this have created circumstances where Rishika ended up killing Sara?"

Dr Neelam swallowed hard, her voice trembling slightly. "You might be right, ACP. Sometimes, Sara went too far with her jokes, but she never meant any harm. I warned her to be careful, but things... they unfolded this way."

ACP stood before the commissioner and said, "Sir, it was the night Ramesh Reddy was killed in his house. Rishika shot him."

The commissioner nodded, his face unreadable. Then he turned to Dr. Neelam. "What happened next, Doctor?"

Dr Neelam took a deep breath before speaking. "The next morning, Sara followed my advice. She tried to distance herself from Rishika. But something unusual happened at Rishika's office, and Sara had no choice but to step in and help her."

The commissioner leaned forward, his curiosity growing. "What exactly happened?"

ACP answered with a grave tone. "Sir, that day, Sub-Inspector Vijay went to Rishika's office for a routine inquiry. During his questioning, Rishika broke down completely. She started crying uncontrollably, and Sara, just as Dr. Neelam said, stepped in to comfort her.

The commissioner's voice softened. "Doctor, you called Rishika on Sunday, 11th October. Was that the last time you spoke to her?"

Dr Neelam shook her head. "No, I called her again on the 13th. She was at work. I told her I wanted to meet her and suggested she bring her boyfriend, Chirag, along. I told her she could introduce me as her aunt."

The commissioner frowned. "But Chirag wasn't real. He only existed in her mind. How did you plan to meet him?"

Dr Neelam's expression turned serious. "I wanted Rishika to trust me. I believed that by accepting her reality, I could help her heal. It's a method I use with patients like her."

The commissioner pressed further. "And did you meet her?"

Dr Neelam sighed, her voice breaking. "No, I couldn't. I had a flight to Dubai on the 13th, so I scheduled our meeting for the weekend. But... before the weekend, everything fell apart. I never imagined something this horrible could happen in just two days. I can't even explain how sorry I feel for Sara." Tears welled up in her eyes as she struggled to finish her words.

The room fell silent for a moment.

The commissioner broke the silence. "Dr. Neelam, you spoke to Rishika on Tuesday, the 13th. Can you tell me what happened between Rishika and Sara after that day?"

Dr Neelam replied, "Their relationship seemed normal as if nothing unusual had happened. In fact, that night, Rishika went to stay with Sara at her flat."

The commissioner raised an eyebrow. "Rishika went to Sara's flat? Why would she do that?"

Before Dr. Neelam could answer, the ACP interrupted. "Sir, on Tuesday the 13th, Rishika called the police control room and gave a tip about the killer of Ramesh. Based on her information, we launched a search operation in the entire Brookfield area. During the operation, we reached Blue Sky Apartments, where Rishika lived. Her landlord told us she wasn't there and was staying with a friend."

"With the landlord's spare key, we searched Rishika's flat. We also checked the neighboring flat, which used to belong to Chirag, also known as Saumitra. The landlord mentioned that the flat remained untouched after Chirag's suicide. No one wanted to rent it because of the tragedy. Later, the landlord told us Rishika had called him during the raid, asking about the police searching Chirag's flat."

The commissioner turned back to Dr. Neelam.

"Doctor, did anything strange happen in Sara's flat that night?"

Dr Neelam hesitated before answering. "Something very strange happened. That night marked the breaking point in their relationship. Sara told me they slept in separate rooms. But the next morning, she found Rishika lying awkwardly on the balcony floor. Sara yelled at her for behaving so oddly. Their fight carried over to the office later that day. It ended with Rishika making heated and ridiculous comments about Sara—and even about me."

ACP began, "Sir, Dr. Neelam is talking about the events of October 14th. That day, something big happened. Rishika had a heated argument with Sara in the conference room. After that, she wasn't the same. She threw things off her desk, yelled at her co-workers, and even spoke rudely to the HR manager. By evening, the company sent her an email putting her on a one-month notice."

"Now, Rishika was talented—especially in coding—and the management didn't want to lose her. The notice was meant as a warning, not a dismissal. But it ended up being her last day. She didn't show up to work the next morning."

The commissioner leaned forward. "You're forgetting something. That same night—October 14th—Rishika was kidnapped by Raj and his gang."

ACP nodded grimly. "Yes, sir. But they let her go after four hours and sent one of Raj's men to keep watch on her. The next night, though, Rishika went to the factory. And that's when the murder happened."

The commissioner's voice turned sharp. "What did Sara tell you after that?"

Dr Neelam spoke softly. "When the goons dragged J.K. away from the office, Sara was shaken. Her instincts told her Rishika had something to do with it, but she had no proof. Desperate to find J.K., Sara went to the factory—and that's where she saw Rishika. She was trying to escape."

Dr Neelam paused, her hands trembling. "Sara didn't tell the police she saw Rishika that night. She wanted answers first. She tried calling Rishika the whole next day, but Rishika's phone was unreachable. Then, on the night of 16th October, Rishika finally called back. Sara confronted her, asking why she was at the factory. Rishika agreed to meet her at her flat."

Dr Neelam's voice broke as tears filled her eyes. "That was the last time Sara saw her. Rishika turned violent, and... and..." She couldn't continue.

The commissioner finished her statement, "So, Rishika strangled Sara with her own hands. Dr Neelam, do you think Rishika realized what she had done in her final days? She didn't just kill Sara—her own friend—but also many others over the last week. Did she understand the weight of her crimes before the end?"

Dr Neelam replied, "It's hard to predict what goes on in someone's mind. But from what I knew of Rishika, deep down, she must have felt guilty. Her suicide speaks to that guilt, though her feelings for Chirag seemed equally strong."

With that, the commissioner sighed and finally closed the case file of Rishika Kapoor, marking the end of a grim chapter.